THE PRACTICAL MAGE'S GUIDE TO MAGIC AND MAYHEM

Dan Ackerman

Supposed Crimes LLC • Matthews, North Carolina

www.supposedcrimes.com

This book is typeset in Goudy Old Style.

For David

GOD HAD graced Hiram Montgomery Reinhart with a life of privilege. He had come into the world as the son of a wealthy planter in southern Georgia. He had chosen to give that away, and though he would not have admitted it, he spent a lot of time regretting that decision. He did not regret freeing the slaves or ending the fighting ring, and he certainly didn't regret buying his niece back from the monster to whom his father had sold her.

He missed the warm weather.

He missed his soft bed and the rich food that Susan had prepared.

He missed having nice things.

In Georgia, he'd had a lot of nice things. A full wardrobe of fine clothes, a feather mattress, and a four-poster bed. He'd eaten off fine China with polished silver. Every luxury paid for in human flesh.

In his new life, luxuries were more than limited; they practically didn't exist. What he did have, he'd bought with coin he'd worked to earn.

Ellen, a girl of six, sat with Hannah, her mother, and Cassie, her grandmother, at the table. She played with her only doll as the two women mended clothes. They all worked, the women doing what domestic work they could find and Hiram selling his services as a mage.

On the plantation, Ellen would have worked, too. Chores all day. She would have cared for Hiram's children, her own cousins, if Hiram had ever married. Here, she didn't worry about things like that.

Hiram didn't want her to work.

He felt bad even making her sit down for reading lessons when she didn't want to do them. Sometimes, he made her, but most of the time, he agreed to let her play a little longer or consented to read her a story instead. She would follow along as he read; sometimes she even giggled when he did voices.

He felt he had to do voices. His mother had always done voices.

He wondered if anyone would remember his birthday. He would be twenty-six on August seventh, which was this coming Friday. It was a greedy thought, but for more than two decades, his birthday had been marked with lavish gifts and a large party where his father hosted other planters, their poised wives and pretty daughters, their haughty sons.

Someone knocked on the door.

Hannah opened it but stepped back just as quickly and said, "Hiram, someone for you." More quietly, she warned, "He stink of magic."

Hannah did not trust mages, as a rule. Hiram did not blame her, considering the way magic had been used at Fall's Hill.

He went to the door, looked over the man, who must have been about ten years his senior, and asked, "Mr...Blackwell, correct?"

"You traffic with demons," Blackwell said.

Hiram balked, his eyes widening. The crispness of the statement startled him.

"Everyone knows it."

"Um. Perhaps you should come inside so that we might speak privately," Hiram suggested.

The man stepped inside, glancing at the other three. He

was not as tall as Hiram, most people weren't, but he was broader-framed, with pale skin and slate gray eyes.

"It is Blackwell, is it not?" Hiram asked.

"Mathew Blackwell," the man said. "You're Hiram Reinhart. You traffic with demons."

Hiram cleared his throat and checked the urge to run his hands through his curls. "I wouldn't say I traffic with them, but there are some unnatural creatures that I have gotten to know."

"I require your assistance in finding one."

"I...uh."

"Or give me the book you use to summon and bind them," the man said. "Your presence is of no consequence."

"Ellen, come on into the other room," Cassie said to her granddaughter. She stood and headed toward the kitchen.

Ellen looked at her grandmother for a moment. Hiram thought she might refuse, but she took her doll and walked away.

Hannah followed them.

"Come sit," Hiram said, gesturing to the now-vacated table. "We can talk."

"There is not much to talk about."

Hiram went to the table.

Blackwell followed him.

They sat across from each other, and Hiram folded his hands on the table, hoping it would disguise his nervousness. He did not know Blackwell as anything more than an acquaintance. He disliked that he had developed a reputation for dealing with unsavory beings. Not that Hiram found inhuman creatures unsavory, by and large, but most people did.

"Who told you that you should seek my help?" Hiram asked.

"Your name came up," Blackwell replied.

"That's vague."

"Julian Candace," Blackwell said tiredly.

"Oh."

"He says he's seen you with some horned creature. Some blue monster. That points towards fey or demons and given your family's reputation, I feel safe betting on demons."

"That was only once, and I've been warned against doing it again," Hiram said. "Besides, he's not the kind of demon you summon to have unpleasant things done."

"I already know the creature I'm looking for. I need help finding it. And you can summon them. Your help or the book, I'm not leaving without one of them."

Hiram did not manage to keep his hand from running through his hair this time, sending the brown locks astray from their careful arrangement. "Why?"

"It doesn't matter."

"It matters a lot. All sorts of things can be done if you have a creature bound to your will. There's a reason it's a closely guarded spell."

"I don't want to bind one," Blackwell stated. "I want to kill one."

Hiram did not know what to say.

"It took my wife. I'll see the thing ended."

Scrambling for time, Hiram asked, "Which demon do you seek? Give me a name."

"I don't need your permission—"

"No, but you do need something I have." Hiram sat up straighter.

"It calls itself Phaedrus."

Hiram said, "I'll look into it and contact you with my decision."

"That's not acceptable."

Hiram stood, straightened his waistcoat, and went over to the door. He opened it and asked, "Is there a way that's best to contact you?"

"I am not leaving without that for which I brought myself to this...place." Gray eyes swept over the room. His lip curled.

"May I remind you that this place is my home, and if you're refusing to leave, I wouldn't be remiss in using force to get you to do so," Hiram said, trying to keep his voice even.

Trying to sound like his father.

Blackwell stood but did not move towards the door.

Hiram, out of the corner of his eye, caught Ellen's small, brown face peering out from the doorway between the main room and the kitchen.

Blackwell remained where he was.

Hiram began to whisper a spell, calling up power to twist around the other mage.

"Stop!" the man called, stepping towards Hiram. "I will be back tomorrow, and you'll help me then, whatever you decide."

Hiram opened the door wider.

Blackwell pushed through it.

Hiram closed it behind him and closed his eyes. He leaned against the door and took a breath.

"Uncle?" Ellen asked.

"Yes, dear?" he asked, turning to face her.

"Is he going to hurt us?"

"No," Hiram said. "Don't worry."

She nodded.

Hiram expected that she would worry anyway.

"Nanny says you shouldn't deal with those sorts."

"Don't worry, Ellie," he said, "We'll be all right."

"Are you sure?"

"I will keep you safe," he said.

She regarded him with dark eyes that shone like bits of obsidian, then turned away and went back to her mother's side. She still did not trust him, and he could not blame her; he was sure she only called him Uncle because he had asked her to.

She had been very young before her father's death, and Hiram had not been much involved in her life until it had fallen on him to return her to her family. After that, she had been sent away with Cassie and Hannah to wait for him. He wondered if the three of them had been happier without him.

He went to kneel beside her. He put a hand on her shoulder, so small and fragile beneath his palm. "I will always do whatever it takes to keep you safe. I promise."

She nodded.

"Don't I keep my promises?"

"Sometimes."

He laughed. "What promises don't I keep?"

"You said I could have a friend to keep Dolly company."

He grinned. "Have you ever been told that patience is a virtue?"

"No."

"I'm very sure I said it to you last week."

She wrinkled her nose.

He gave her shoulder the gentlest of squeezes. "You may say I broke my promise if I don't deliver by Christmas. Is that fair?"

"That's fair," her grandmother answered for her.

Hiram stood. He scanned the room until his eyes settled on his jacket. He almost always put it somewhere different. He retrieved it from where he'd placed it and pulled it on.

When he opened the door, Cassie asked, "Where you headed?"

"I'm going to speak to a friend. I hope to be back soon."

She nodded.

He set down the road and made several turns, out of the area where he lived and toward the nicer part of Pickering where Julian lived. If Hiram had lived alone, he could have lived in this part of town as well, as Julian was not a better mage than he was.

Even if he had passed off the women as servants instead of family, they would have been able to secure better housing, but that was not the choice he'd made.

He knocked on Julian's door, and his sister, a woman a few years younger than Hiram, answered. She smiled when she saw him and said, "Oh, Mr. Reinhart, what surprise. I'm sure my brother will be so glad that you've called. Please come in."

"Thank you, Miss Candace," he said as he entered.

"I'll go get him."

Julian could usually be found in his study. He worked

hard, taking on extra jobs and projects. Hiram doubted he needed to do it to survive, but Julian liked to keep his family comfortable.

Hiram waited just inside the door.

Julian entered, tidy and well-dressed, without his sister, and said, "Come in, don't be a stranger."

Hiram took a few steps further in.

Julian gestured for him to follow. The other man led Hiram to his study, where they sat and Julian asked, "What can I do for you, Hiram?"

Hiram's initial instinct, as it always was when speaking to Julian, was to say something kind. He liked Julian a lot, more than he should have, and had to remind himself not to act like a girl who wanted to be courted.

"You've given someone my name," Hiram said.

"I did. Perhaps it wasn't my place, but I assumed that with so many mouths to feed, you wouldn't balk at extra work," answered the blond mage.

"I'd rather not have it spread that I deal with demons."

"You do deal with demons, Hiram," Julian said practically.

"June is the only one I know personally, and he is not that sort of demon."

Julian rolled his eyes, beautiful honey-colored eyes, and said, "Fallen angels or Devil's spawn, they are all the same sort of demon. Monsters."

Hiram shook his head but did not argue. It did his reputation no good to defend the kindness of unholy creatures.

"One demon is more than most mages of our level know anyway," Julian said. "I thought you would be the man for the job."

Hiram sighed.

"What?" Julian asked. "I didn't think you'd be this upset. I didn't think you'd be upset at all, truth be told."

"Blackwell...he's very insistent that I either help him kill this creature or turn over my books so that he can do it alone."

"Kill it?" Julian asked, his brow knitting. "He said he wanted to find it."

"I don't like to kill things, Julian. It sits poorly with me."

"Have you killed someone?" Julian asked.

"Things, Julian. And it sat poorly."

"And I don't imagine you'd turn over your books?"

"They have been in my family since before the Americas were settled by Europeans. I'm *not* handing them over to anyone."

"You're going to tell him you won't help," Julian guessed.

"Yes."

"And you think he'll take your answer poorly."

"Yes. He came to my home."

Julian tapped the table. He thought for a while, then advised, "Send a note, tell him to meet you somewhere public. I'll come with you. I know Mathew rather well. He should listen to me."

"Thank you, Julian. I owe you a favor."

"If you want to do me a favor, you can marry my sister," Julian said.

Hiram felt his face grow hot and knew he had blushed. "What?"

"Cora just ended her *third* engagement. Father would never have stood for it, but she's got Mother wrapped around her finger. She's love-struck for a few months, engaged for a week, and then suddenly she can't stand him anymore. Driving me mad. And it isn't good for her reputation."

"I don't see how you think she'd treat me any different."

"Oh, I don't. I was joking. You take everything so seriously, Hiram."

He blushed again.

Julian smiled. "It's one of the things I like about you. You've got a good head on your shoulders. You understand what it means to be responsible for something, not like the others."

"Others?" Hiram asked.

"You know, the other mages our age. Frivolous and silly, more concerned with showing off."

Hiram nodded.

"And Mother is always asking me when I'm going to marry Angeline, as though I don't have a hard enough time saving for that and supporting her and Cora," Julian said, then immediately looked reticent. "I shouldn't complain about all this."

Hiram shifted. "I imagine that's a burden."

"You're doing it right, Hiram, waiting. I don't know what everyone's hurry is."

Hiram almost laughed at the idea that he was waiting to be engaged to anyone.

"Anyway, tomorrow. Set the meeting for one, let's say. Come get me before you go," Julian said.

Hiram nodded. "Thank you again."

THE FOLLOWING day, a little after noon, Hiram went to Julian's home. They walked together to the meeting house, where Hiram had asked Blackwell to meet him. When they arrived, they saw that Blackwell had not come alone.

Hiram had feared as much.

"Don't look so nervous," Julian advised as they approached the three men that waited for them.

"I can't help it," he said but said nothing more as they drew closer.

"Mr. Reinhart," Blackwell greeted them. "And Mr. Candace. I'm surprised to see you."

"Oh, Mr. Reinhart and I had some business to attend to afterward, I thought I could keep him company," Julian said, calm and pleasant.

Hiram shifted, straightening his waistcoat.

"Have you come to your decision?"

Hiram nodded. He smoothed his waistcoat again, though it hadn't moved since last time. As a child, he'd twirled his hair and chewed his nails, habits his father had frightened out of him. His clothes had taken the brunt of his fidgeting since. "I can't abide helping you take a life, and I cannot risk giving you my family's books. You'll have to seek assistance somewhere else."

"I've told you before, that's unacceptable," Blackwell said.

"Come now, I'm sure there's something else you can do," Julian said. "There are many mages, in this town and others. Mr. Reinhart's been quite clear."

Blackwell shook his head. The men he'd brought glanced between each other.

Hiram took a step backward.

"Don't involve yourself in this," Blackwell warned.

"I'm afraid it's too late," Julian said.

"I lost my *wife*," Blackwell said to Julian. "What would you do if someone took Miss Hoffman from you?"

Julian hesitated and looked at Hiram for a moment. "I...I don't know."

"You don't understand," Blackwell told him. He turned back to Hiram. "Help me."

"I can't," Hiram said.

Blackwell looked at the men who had accompanied him, then around the meeting house. "This isn't done." He turned and walked away.

"I don't think that went well," Hiram said.

"No, me neither," Julian said; he glanced after then men, his mouth twisted with concern. "I thought he'd be angrier...walking away, that isn't like him."

"No?"

"Normally you can...well, you can fight with him to make him see reason. But walking away? I feel bad for the thing he's after."

"I should go home."

"Why? I don't think he'd go after your family."

"No. I have to talk to someone."

Julian frowned at him. "At home?"

"Um. Yes."

"Who?"

"Just a friend."

Julian's eyebrows raised. "I believed your limited circle of friends stands before you. Unless those women you live with–"

"My family," Hiram said.

"Yes, well," Julian said, "My family is all women too, and I don't like to trouble them with matters like this."

"It's a different friend."

"A demon?" Julian asked.

"Shh," Hiram said.

"Can I come? I've never seen one, not in real life."

"I'm not summoning him," Hiram said and hoped it would be the end of it. He headed toward home.

Julian followed him, despite Hiram's lack of consent.

At home, Hiram took their largest bowl from the kitchen and filled it with water. He set it on the table, took a knife, and rolled up his sleeve.

"Hiram," Julian said. He stared at the exposed skin of Hiram's forearm, then the blade in his hand.

"It's part of the spell."

The other mage didn't look comforted. "What kind of spell?"

"I haven't been able to work out a better way to make cross-temporal contact," Hiram explained, tightening his grip on the knife handle. "This spell needs blood."

"But...to summon the creature, would that also require blood?"

"No."

"So why not summon the creature?" Julian asked.

"He doesn't like being summoned," Hiram said. The answer left out a larger truth, which was that the June that lived in Hiram's present would have sooner spit on him than speak to him. The June Hiram contacted now, the one in the future, had softened his stance on Hiram.

Hiram gritted his teeth then drew the knife across his arm. He hoped he would not cry out, especially with Julian watching.

He thanked God for the sharpness of Cassie's knives. The blade sliced his arm cleanly, with nothing more than a throb and a sting.

He dabbled his fingers in the thin dribble of blood. He smeared it on the bowl and himself, chanting the words June had taught him.

A face appeared in the bowl, blue-skinned and horned. "Hiram!" the face cried, pleasantly surprised but ultimately unphased.

June had visited once, and only once before he'd informed Hiram that it was best not to stay in contact. Nothing personal, he'd assured, and had alluded to some kind of trouble with an authority of which Hiram had never heard.

"Hello, June," he said.

Julian crowded close to him, peering into the bowl.

Hiram tried to breathe normally.

June asked, "What are you doing in my coffee?"

"I wanted to ask you about another of your kind."

"Sure, I love to gossip. Who?"

"Phaedrus."

"Phaedrus? What could have happened with Phaedrus?"

"A mage is after the creature, revenge for harming his wife."

"No, Phaedrus is a storyteller, not violent at all. Who's that with you?" June asked, his tone heavy with implication.

Hiram's face grew hot. "This is Julian. He's a friend."

June grinned. "I hope so."

The bowl began to shake.

"I guess you've got to go," June said. "I'd check in with Phaedrus, give a warning, at least."

"Thank you, June."

"Bye, Hiram, take care!" June said pleasantly. "I honestly do wish I could visit."

Hiram ended the spell.

The demon's face disappeared.

Julian remained by Hiram's side for a moment, peering into the now inert water. He noted, "It's not a very good spell, is it?"

"No," Hiram admitted. "But talking across time is

difficult."

Julian nodded and stepped back. "So. Do you believe him?" He handed Hiram a rag and indicated the blood on Hiram's face.

Hiram scrubbed at the blood. "I do."

"You don't think he's lying to protect his own? You missed a spot, right here." Julian tapped his own face to show position.

"No."

Julian regarded him for a moment. "You truly believe him. How do you know him?"

"It's a long story."

"I don't have anywhere else to be," Julian said.

Hiram sighed. "My grandfather summoned him, took him captive, and my family held him for fifty years, forcing him to fight for the entertainment of others."

Julian's honey eyes clouded. "Your family ran a fighting ring?"

"It's not something of which I'm proud," Hiram pointed out. He did his best not to sulk. Pouting didn't look good on a child, let alone a man of his age.

"I hate to ask, but...if your family had him captive, do you really think he's on your side?" Julian asked. "I would certainly bear someone ill will."

"June has my trust, completely," he said.

Julian said nothing.

Hiram went into his bedroom and found the book he needed, then returned to the kitchen with it. He set it on the kitchen table and began to gather the things he would need for the spell.

Julian went over to the book and flipped through. "This is it? The book your family passed down."

"One of three."

"It doesn't look old."

"Precautions were taken to protect them from age and elements," Hiram said without a glance at the book.

"What are you doing?"

"I'm going to locate Phaedrus and hopefully figure out what actually happened. If June says he's not a killer, then there must be something else going on." He took the map he had found and spread it over the table.

"Don't get involved in this," Julian advised.

Hiram looked at him. "I'm already involved in this. Because you gave him my name, I should remind you."

Julian frowned, his mouth tugging down.

Hiram stared at his mouth for a second, wanting to say something to make him smile. He liked to see Julian smile, even though it wasn't his place; the man had a fiancée.

"I'll help you get out of this, Hiram," Julian said. "Since I am to blame," he added with a smile.

Hiram nodded and returned to his work, flipping through the book to locate the spell he needed.

"Is the spell written in a long-form *script?*" Julian asked. He tapped the paragraph where the instructions ended and the incantation began.

"Old-fashioned, I know, but it's needed for this type of work," Hiram said. "I don't dare fiddle with it."

"No, I don't blame you. What if he's not on the map?" Julian asked. He peered over Hiram's shoulder and began to help. He fell easily into a rhythm with Hiram to prepare the spell, painting the required symbols and arranging the items as needed.

Hiram took a small marble and placed it on the map. "The marble will roll off the map if the creature isn't within its bounds," Hiram said.

He lifted the book and read over the words he would need to chant, going over it to make sure he wouldn't stumble. He took a breath and began the spell, eyes trained on the page. When he finished, he looked up to see both Julian and Ellen staring at him. His niece had inched into the room to stand right beside him, her little face tilted up.

"Ellen, get outta there, you let your uncle do his work," Cassie said, coming into the room and taking the little girl by the hand.

Ellen pulled her hand back. "I want to watch."

Cassie stared down at her.

Hiram glanced at Cassie, who crossed her arms.

"The spell's all done, Ellie," he said.

"You never let me watch you do spells," the girl accused.

"I didn't know you wanted to watch," he said.

"Mama and Nanny says I can't."

"No good to be fooling around with," Cassie warned.

"Oh, Hiram, looks like you've found an apprentice," Julian teased.

Hiram smiled. He hadn't been any older than Ellen when his mother had begun to teach him magic. "First we'll have to work on reading, then we'll see about magic," Hiram told his niece.

She smiled a real smile, one that crinkled the corners of her eyes and showed her dimples. Ellen had two smiles; one for being polite to strangers, a smile that made people think she was shy and obedient instead of waiting to be released from their company. The other smile he saw occasionally, most often when he caved to her requests for a bedtime story.

Cassie took her by the hand and led her out of the room.

Julian peered down at the map and said, "The creature is in Pickering."

Hiram came over beside him. "So he is."

"Should we go?"

"I suppose we should," Hiram said, suddenly nervous about the venture he had undertaken. June hadn't lied to him, he believed that, but he wasn't infallible. He could be wrong. This could be a dangerous creature or at least, one already embroiled in dangerous happenings.

"Come along, I know that neighborhood fairly well," Julian said. "I think I even recall that boarding house."

He walked away, and Hiram followed him.

As he walked through the district in which Phaedrus resided with Julian in a confident lead, Hiram wondered how it had come to be that Julian knew this area. Young men of certain standing did sometimes go to rougher neighborhoods to take in the sights; Hiram had not thought Julian among them, given his fiancée and family commitments. Maybe he'd been wrong.

Hiram peeled his eyes away from a lady of the evening. He caught up with Julian and asked, "Are you sure you know where we're going?"

"Yes," Julian assured, "I've got a very good sense of direction." He paused before a boarding house, glanced at Hiram, then stepped inside. He walked up to the desk in the common room and said, "Excuse me, I'm looking for someone."

The man behind the desk looked at him. "Doesn't much concern me, does it?"

"We can pay for information," Julian offered.

"And my customers have paid for confidence." The man prickled.

Hiram had not intended to pay for anything. "We don't

have ill intentions, we come to warn someone. A demon by the name of Phaedrus. Please."

The man behind the desk looked concerned for a moment, then beckoned a young woman over. He whispered something to her; she nodded and left. To them, the man said, "You can wait here."

"Thank you," Julian said.

"Have a seat," the man said, gesturing to a settee against the wall.

They sat and a few minutes later, the young woman returned. She said nothing to them and resumed her cleaning.

Several more minutes passed.

Hiram began to wonder if they should leave, but a robe-clad figure stepped into the room, marked clearly as one of the Fallen by jade-colored skin. Only fairies and Fallen had skin in those tones and the creature lacked the ethereal, volatile air of the fey.

The creature approached without looking particularly impressed but not especially annoyed at their presence.

Julian and Hiram stood.

"Phaedrus?" Hiram asked, trying not to stare too much.

"That's me," said the creature, who stood about as tall as Hiram. "You wanted to speak to me."

Hiram nodded.

"Something better discussed in private, I'm sure," Phaedrus said, "Follow me."

They followed. Julian leaned close to Hiram and whispered, "I thought we were after a man."

The demon glanced back at them. "And you don't think you've found one?"

With color going to his cheeks, Julian responded, "I didn't mean any offense."

"No, no, I understand. Most humans have grown so strict with their delineations," Phaedrus conceded tiredly, stopping before a door and opening it. "Please come in."

They entered the room.

The creature gestured for them to sit and took a seat on

the bed, legs folded. "Tell me what you've come for," Phaedrus said.

Julian and Hiram stared.

Finally, Hiram cleared his throat and said, "A man named Mathew Blackwell is after you. He says you killed his wife."

"Certainly not!" Phaedrus said. "I'm no murderer."

"That's what June said," Hiram said.

"June?" The creature's eyebrow quirked up.

"Junius—"

"Thompson, yes, I know who he is." Phaedrus waved away Hiram's answer. "Is he in town?"

"No, I contacted him."

Phaedrus nodded. "Do you believe that I am in danger?"

"Blackwell wants you dead," Julian answered. "He tried to enlist Mr. Reinhart's help to do it."

The creature's moon-colored eyes widened. "I suppose I am in danger, then. Thank you for letting me know. I will be decidedly more careful."

"But his wife," Julian insisted before the creature could dismiss them. "Something must have happened for him to be after you."

"Oh, I did take his wife, but only to bring her to safety. She's expecting a child that isn't his," Phaedrus said.

"You'll be able to take care of yourself?" Hiram asked.

Phaedrus smiled, stood, and walked towards the door. "I usually manage. Thank you, again, gentlemen, for warning me. Let me see you out."

The two men stood. Julian hesitated, plainly observing the creature, as he had been for several minutes.

"What?" Phaedrus asked. The politeness from before slipped marginally.

"What *are* you?" Julian asked with curious wonder.

Hiram balked. Every instinct demanded he apologize for his friend, but Julian's behavior mortified him so badly he couldn't think.

"Phaedrus Queen, malak ha-satan, among the first fallen," the creature said, "though I expect that's not the answer you wanted."

"I...you're just..." Julian stumbled. "Unusual. Looking."

Hiram wished he hadn't pried.

"Are all demons like that?"

"I'm not a man," Phaedrus explained with a weariness that spoke of deep familiarity with this conversation, "Or a woman. I was not made to live in a body. I won't be held to any standard because I ended up with one."

"Oh," Julian said.

"They," Phaedrus said.

"What?" Julian asked.

"Use they or them in reference to me," the demon requested pleasantly. "Though I don't expect we'll see each other again."

Phaedrus opened the door.

The two men exited.

Hiram tried to give Phaedrus an apologetic look, but he might have just grimaced at them.

On the way out, Julian babbled a lot about what he thought Phaedrus could be, what type of demon they were, why they had fallen, and if they trafficked regularly with the Devil. He also guessed as to what their physical form was like, exactly, if they had some sexual variation or deformity.

"Julian," Hiram interrupted after several minutes of uneasy listening, "If the creature had wanted you to know, they would have told you."

"I...I wonder, is all. There's no malice in wondering!" Julian insisted.

"You have a fiancée," Hiram reminded. "You should not be wondering about other people in such a way."

"That's a point I must concede, Angeline would certainly be upset," the other mage agreed thoughtfully.

They walked together for several minutes, then, without warning, Julian asked, "Now that Phaedrus has been warned, what's our next step?"

"What do you mean?"

"I'm still concerned about what Blackwell might do."

Hiram nodded. "I'll be on guard, that's for sure."

"Perhaps your family would be safer elsewhere, for a little while, at least. Is there somewhere you can send them?"

The idea sent a shiver through him; he hadn't considered that. He had spent too much of his life sheltered and immune to threats by virtue of his social standing. Hiram thought for a moment, then nodded. "Yes."

"And they'll go?"

"If they think Ellen might be in danger, they won't hesitate."

Julian patted his back. "I'm sure all will be well soon enough. Blackwell is surely overacting. Maybe he's assuming his wife is dead. It could all be a misunderstanding."

They parted ways. Julian headed toward his home and Hiram toward his.

Hiram found Hannah at the table, sewing. He said, not sure how else to start, "I think you should go to visit Susan."

Hannah looked up. "Is there trouble?" she asked softly so that Ellen wouldn't hear; the girl was in the kitchen making dinner with her grandmother.

"A little. Maybe."

"With that man who came here?"

"Yes."

She nodded and stood. "For a long time?"

"I don't expect so," he said, going to the kitchen. He went to a cabinet and took down a sack of beans, then pressed his hand to the bare wood in the cabinet, whispering a spell. A small square of wood slid away. He reached into the compartment to take out all the extra money they had saved. A penny here and there. Sometimes a whole dollar if they'd encountered some kind of windfall.

While Hannah and Cassie packed their own things, he helped Ellen pack. As they packed, the child was quiet, almost dour. As he latched close the suitcase, she sat on the bed and regarded him with her mouth turned down.

"What's that face for?" he asked.

"Do we have to go away for a long time?"

"I don't know. I hope not." The house, small as it was, would echo without them.

"Why aren't you coming?"

"I have things to take care of here."

"Work?"

He nodded and put a hand on her shoulder. "Yes. I'll write."

"Do you promise?"

"I do."

They stayed to eat dinner. When the meal was finished, he handed over the money.

"Safe travels," he wished them. "I'll send a letter when it's time to come home."

"Why do we have to go?" Ellen asked.

"The air here isn't any good for you," Hiram said, "A visit to Susan will do your lungs well."

"I don't *like* the country. Susan makes me find eggs."

"Be good," he said.

"Yes, Uncle," she said.

He wondered how much of her obedience was nothing but a reflex from the time when she had been owned. "And have fun, Ellie, you'll be able to go swimming and run around in the fields. Maybe there will be kittens."

She smiled at the mention of kittens, a real smile. "If there are kittens, can I keep one?"

"They won't be my kittens. You'll have to ask Susan."

"Watch out for yourself," Hannah said.

"I will," he said.

Cassie patted his arm on the way out.

Once they had gone, the house felt empty and quiet. He struggled to get to sleep that night.

HIRAM SPENT three days undisturbed, heading each day to the workshop where mages convened and doing little else. He began to grow hopeful that Blackwell had simply given up; it seemed too much to hope for, but he liked to hope.

He excelled at hoping. He could always find some way to hope things would work out in his favor. Things usually did.

As he cast a charm for good health on his fifth ring for the day, he decided that if a week went by and nothing happened, that he would write for the women to return. Someone tapped him on the shoulder and told him it was time to clean up.

He tidied his workspace, dreaming idly of the spells he had been able to work before he had left home; they had been spells for entertainment, for curiosity, not enchantments he would sell for money.

He handed in the rings he had enchanted. After an inspection, the woman seated at the desk counted out his pay and handed it to him. He pocketed it and headed for the door. On his walk home, he bought himself something hot from a street vendor, not in the mood to cook dinner that night; his skills in the kitchen were not excellent, and he didn't fancy another omelet.

He ate as he walked, wondering if his parents would be appalled at where his life had brought him. His father would be, he knew that much, but he didn't know enough of his mother to guess what her opinion would have been.

The door to his home opened at his touch and he stepped back, his stomach turning violently. He listened, but heard nothing; when he hesitantly stepped inside, he found the house ransacked.

He rushed to the bedroom and found all three volumes of the books Blackwell had wanted missing, plucked from the trunk where he kept his small collection of tomes. He knelt before the trunk for a moment, cursing himself for not being more careful.

He hurried back outside, intending to seek Julian's advice, but once he stepped outside the door, something hit him in the face, something dense. It smelled otherworldly. It felt like a small down pillow, and he caught it as it tumbled from his face down his chest, leaving a trail of orange powder.

It looked like a small pillow as well.

He looked around to see who had thrown it, but he grew too woozy. When he tried to take a step, his knees went weak. He found his tongue swollen and unable to produce the sounds he needed for a spell.

He crumpled to the ground, unable to control his body. Someone lifted him, the same one who had thrown the pillow into his face, and threw him over their shoulder. He lost his sight and consciousness before they had gone three yards from the house.

He woke when he was dropped to the floor; it jostled him through his whole body and made him bite his tongue. He groaned.

"I didn't want him," he heard Blackwell tell someone.

"He came home, figured it was better this way," the man who had taken him said.

Blackwell scoffed, then said, "Fine. You retrieved the books?"

"I did."

Hiram sat up.

"Quick, deal with him before he tries something." Blackwell grabbed the sack from the other man's hands and dumped the books on the table.

The man, of a dark complexion and younger than Hiram, shoved a gag into Hiram's mouth and pushed Hiram on to his stomach. He put a knee in the small of his back and roughly tied his hands.

The man's weight blessedly lifted before Hiram could suffocate.

Hiram tried to sit up, wriggling first onto his side.

"Stay down if you wish to remain unharmed," Blackwell warned.

Hiram stopped moving, gagging a little as he swallowed the blood that seeped from his tongue. He breathed slowly, knowing that if he vomited, he would likely choke to death on it. He watched Blackwell open the first volume, reading the first page for several minutes, then leafing through the rest of the book.

"It can't all be this dense," Blackwell said to himself. "And no index!" He tossed it down.

Hiram winced.

After a moment more of scowling at the book, Blackwell turned to look at Hiram. "You know these books."

Hiram stared up at him, still hazy and now feeling ill from the blood he had swallowed. His body ached, especially his mouth. He might die here, choking on regurgitated blood and street food.

Grim thought, that. He tried to clear it from his mind.

"Maybe it was a stroke of luck that Eddie took you," Blackwell said thoughtfully. He knelt beside Hiram, who did his best to scoot away from him. Blackwell reached over and grabbed him by one arm. He pulled him to the table and him onto the bench. "Go ahead."

Hiram stared up at him and then glanced down at the gag; he didn't intend to help Blackwell, but if he took the gag off, he might be able to get out a quick spell.

Blackwell reached for the gag, then pulled back.

"Eddie!" he called.

The dark-skinned young man reappeared. "Yes?"

"Put him in the cell we made for that thing, then go down to Franklin's and buy a cuff."

"A cuff?" Eddie asked.

"He'll know what you're talking about. For a mage, not a creature."

Eddie nodded and lifted Hiram by the arm more gently than Blackwell had. He walked him into a small room that must have started life as a storage closet because, in addition to reeking of magic, it also smelled of starch and lye.

Eddie closed the door on him.

Hiram was left in the dark; he sat on the bare floor, leaning uncomfortably against the wall.

He heard Eddie and Blackwell speaking to each other, their voices muffled by the door and possibly by magic.

He tried to work at his bonds but did nothing but chafe the skin on his wrists until it was raw. His throat tightened, and an ache spread through his chest; he began to sniffle and then to weep.

Tears, snot, spit, and blood soaked the rag. The dampness of the rag seeped into his skin, leaving it waterlogged around his mouth.

By the time Eddie returned, Hiram had lapsed into a hollow panic. He winced at the light of the lantern the man brought with him.

Eddie brought him forward, loosened his bonds, and placed a metal cuff onto his wrist. The cuff sealed itself with a surge of heat and singed Hiram's skin.

Eddie reached up and pulled the gag from Hiram's mouth. "Try a spell."

"What?" he croaked.

"Try a spell, got to make sure that thing works," Eddie said.

Hiram tried a spell, and nothing happened.

"It works," Eddie called out to Blackwell.

"Bring him out," Blackwell ordered.

Eddie sat Hiram at the table.

Blackwell pushed the books towards him. "Find me the spells for summoning."

Hiram shook his head.

"Find me the spell and you're free," Blackwell offered.

"You're after a creature that hasn't done anything. Your wife is alive."

"I'm after a thing that took my whore of a wife from me. I'll make it tell me where she is, and then I'll deal with both of them."

"I won't help you do that," Hiram said, shaking his head. He understood why Blackwell's wife had needed help to get away from her husband.

"You'll rethink soon enough," Blackwell said, giving Hiram a friendly pat on the shoulder. He pulled the first volume back over and opened the book to the page he had marked. He had not read more than a dozen pages; it was dense reading.

Hiram knew that it would take him several weeks, maybe a month to go through each volume unless he was an exceptional reader.

Knowing that the spell he sought was halfway through the second volume, Hiram estimated a month and a half before he found the spell he sought if he read each spell all the way through.

Hiram did not think he would read all the spells; he thought Blackwell would give up on the spells he didn't need.

Two weeks, maybe, Hiram thought as he amended his estimates. Maybe Blackwell would kill him sooner; he knew he wasn't going to be set free.

Or he could find the spell for him. That could buy him freedom if he was lucky, but it would surely condemn Phaedrus and the unfortunate Mrs. Blackwell.

"You look like you're thinking hard, Mr. Reinhart," Blackwell said.

"I don't feel well," Hiram said, which was true. He felt terrible.

"Hmm, that's a shame," Blackwell said.

Hiram pushed himself up from the table.

"Where are you going?"

"If you're going to kill me, do it," Hiram said, "Whatever you're going to do, do it. Otherwise, I'm going to lie down."

Blackwell made a thoughtful sound and didn't make any move to stop him.

Hiram curled up in the closet-turned-cell and didn't fall asleep as much as he passed out. Hours later, someone threw something on top of him. He sat up, groggy but frightened, and saw Eddie standing over him, illuminated ominously by the lantern he had set down.

"I'm not allowed to give you food," Eddie said. He dropped a pillow onto his lap and held out a mug of water. "Water isn't food."

Hiram took it and guzzled it. He returned the mug and caught his breath, panting uncouthly. He asked, "You work for Blackwell?"

"After a fashion."

"What do you mean?"

Eddie unbuttoned his shirt, which seemed strange until Hiram saw something gleaming in his chest. He took up the lantern and stood, staring at the chunk of glass that had been lodged in his chest, the flesh growing around it.

"Mr. Blackwell's magic is the only thing that keeps me alive," Eddie said.

Hiram nodded. "I believe I understand, then."

Eddie nodded as well. "If you can find a way...if you can undo his plans, it'd be best. He's got a vicious streak."

"I hope I can."

Eddie took the lantern back and stepped out of the doorway. "Goodnight."

"Goodnight. Thank you," he said. He stepped back into the cell to allow Eddie to close the door.

He arranged the pillow and blanket and returned to sleep; the days to come would be unpleasant, he was sure, and he hoped for a night of happy dreams.

IN THE morning, Eddie opened the door but said nothing.

Blackwell peered down at him and asked, "Have you changed your mind yet, Mr. Reinhart?"

"No."

"Very well. Join me for breakfast," he said.

Eddie stood nearby, ready to physically enforce the request should Hiram decline.

Hiram sat at the table, unwilling to inconvenience Eddie and not particularly wishing to sit in the closet any longer. Sitting at the table of a cold-blooded madman was not much of an improvement, but it was one nevertheless.

Eddie set an empty plate and a mug of water in front of Hiram.

Blackwell had a hearty breakfast on his own plate. He noticed Hiram's gaze. "Eddie can certainly prepare you something if you're willing to cooperate."

Hiram shook his head. "No, thank you." He watched Blackwell eat, sipping at his water. Once Blackwell had eaten and the plates were cleared, Hiram asked, "Is there somewhere I can wash?"

Blackwell eyed him.

"Or at least relieve myself?" Hiram asked.

Blackwell nodded. "Eddie, if you would be so kind."

Eddie brought him up from the basement where they had been and into a house that felt like it should have had a family. It was warm, elegant, and comfortable, part of the façade Blackwell must have needed.

Eddie showed him to a water closet, fully furnished with modern fittings. "Mrs. Blackwell's idea," Eddie said when he saw Hiram marveling at the plumbing. "She was a modern woman."

Hiram nodded.

"Take the time you need," the young man said and stepped out of the doorway.

Hiram relieved himself and washed. He checked in the small mirror and tried to calm the wayward direction of his curls, but he would have little luck without proper hygiene products. He tried to use soap to slip the cuff from his wrist, but it was fruitless, as he had known it would be.

When they returned, Blackwell said, "That took a very long time."

Hiram said nothing.

By lunch, he had a headache, and by dinner, he felt sick. Blackwell came and went throughout the day, taking his meals with Hiram, offering him food on the condition that he help with the spell.

Hiram refused each time, but he went to bed that night with the dreadful feeling that he would cave by lunch the following day. Hunger was not something with which he was accustomed, even now. They may have lacked fine and exotic ingredients, but each member of Hiram's family had as much as they needed on their plates every day.

He went to sleep, but in the middle of the night, Eddie woke him. He tossed Hiram a few scraps of food and said, "Please, don't give in. And don't tell him it was me."

"He'll know you've been sneaking me things if I don't starve," Hiram said.

"I'm just trying to buy time at this point."

Hiram nodded and gobbled down the stale bread, rind of cheese, and carrot greens. He was awake the rest of the night with a stomachache.

The following morning, he watched Blackwell eat breakfast and refused to help.

Blackwell frowned at him and by lunch, he seemed to grow angry. Eddie cleared the plates and Blackwell followed him out of the room.

Eddie returned with ropes in hand, his eyes on the ground. Without saying a word, he bound Hiram's hands and feet to the chair.

Blackwell entered after Hiram had been left to sit for a while. He had a blade with him. Not just a letter opener or a kitchen knife but a thin, wicked blade meant for unpleasant things.

Hiram grew very nervous.

Blackwell set the three books on the table. "I'm done with this game. You're going to help me, now."

Hiram shook his head. "No, I won't. I won't help you kill someone."

"Why do you sympathize with these monsters over your fellow man?" Blackwell asked but didn't wait for an answer. He took the knife and pressed it to Hiram's shoulder.

Hiram squeezed his eyes shut, but penetration never came.

"Hmm...but that would be messy, wouldn't it?" he asked.

Hiram opened his eyes and watched Blackwell bring over a candle and light it with the flick of his wrist and a few words. He put the blade over the flame and held it there for a while. Hiram worked at his bonds and started to sweat, going hot and cold all over. He accomplished nothing.

Blackwell took the blade and pushed aside the collar of Hiram's shirt, exposing the side of his neck. He pressed the flat of the blade against Hiram's flesh and it sizzled.

Hiram screamed and tried to pull away, put Blackwell held on to him.

He pulled the blade back and asked, "Would you like to

help me now?"

Hiram couldn't calm his breathing enough to answer, but he shook his head. He didn't know how long it would take for him to give in.

Blackwell returned the blade to the flame, waiting patiently to it to heat again.

Hiram squeezed his eyes shut, tears leaking down his face. "Please, don't."

"It's a simple request, Mr. Reinhart," Blackwell said. "I can't imagine why you won't cooperate. You've been intolerable since the start, denying me for no reason. I can't stand that, you know, being refused things, especially when they're simple. Will you help me?"

Hiram shook his head again, knowing that he would give in sooner or later, but wanting to last as long as he could. A delay to someone else's demise, a point of pride, the goodness of his heart, or plain Reinhart stubbornness, Hiram didn't know.

Blackwell pulled aside his shirt and pressed the blade to his shoulder, pushing it hard into his flesh. It slid in and burned as it went.

Hiram screamed again, feeling sick and pitiful.

Eddie entered the room.

Blackwell looked up without removing the blade.

"Mr. Blackwell, you have a guest approaching," Eddie informed him. "You may wish to set this aside for a different time."

"Of course, thank you, Eddie." Blackwell tossed the knife on the table and headed toward the door.

"Are you done with him?" Eddie asked, glancing at Hiram.

"No, not at all," Blackwell said and left.

Once he was gone, Eddie untied Hiram and examined the burns. "Not pretty." He half-carried Hiram back to the closet and vowed, "I'll bring you something to eat."

Hiram lay on his back and stared up at the ceiling. "Thank you, Eddie. You're very kind."

Eddie left him there.

Hiram lay for a long time. He knew his wounds were not that severe. They hurt, certainly, but they weren't debilitating; he had seen slaves whipped and back in the fields before they were halfway healed. The human body had an enormous capacity to endure, and that sent fear lacing through him.

Eddie brought him food and a cold cloth to press to his burns. "He'll be with his guest for a while, then he'll be out for the rest of the day. Lucky for us, Mr. Blackwell is a busy man with a full social calendar."

"Lucky for us," Hiram muttered.

Though Hiram had asked nothing of him, Eddie insisted, "I can't let you go. It'd be my life."

"I know," Hiram said. "If you can get my cuff off..."

"I don't know anything about magic, I'm sorry."

"If I told you what I needed?"

"Maybe I could get it. What do you need?"

Hiram snorted vulgarly. "I don't know. Light, for one, to read the runes by. If I can fathom the spell, perhaps I can find a way to undo it."

Eddie nodded. "I'll bring you what I can when I can."

"Thank you."

"You rest up, though," Eddie said. "I've got other work to do. I'll check in later."

Eddie closed the door on him, leaving him in the closet.

Hiram tried to sleep and tried not to let his thoughts become overly dark. He had little luck in either endeavor, though he did quietly entertain the hope that Julian would know where to look for him. If he could hold out until someone realized he was gone, he might survive.

Of course, he'd sent away the only people who would truly note his absence.

By the light of the candle that Eddie brought him, Hiram managed to work out that the cuff could not be removed with magic but required a key. What sort of key he needed or where he would get one, he didn't know.

It didn't seem to matter; three days passed in exactly the same way. Blackwell would come and read. He would turn to cutting, burning, and hitting Hiram for a little while, then returning to his reading. He would alternate between the two, growing bored with one and resuming the other.

He made it through the first book and closed it; he turned his eyes back to Hiram.

"You don't need to do this, any of this," Hiram said.

"Need to? No, of course not, Mr. Reinhart, I *want* to do it," Blackwell said. He stood and approached Hiram, who let out a whimper as soon as he came near. Blackwell smiled and lifted the knife, looking between Hiram and the blade. "Your friend Mr. Candace has been asking about you. He's terribly concerned."

"Leave him out of this."

Blackwell settled on digging the point of the knife into one of the new burns that he had left on Hiram's skin that morning, popping the blister and pressing into the tender skin beneath.

Hiram always thought he had no more screams left, but he cried out every time. This time he let out a sniveling weep.

"It ends if you tell me," Blackwell reasoned, wiping the blade on Hiram's trouser leg and setting it beneath his left eye. "Hazel. My mother had hazel eyes until she grew cataracts. Unsightly things. I can't stand to look her in the face anymore."

He pressed the tip carefully against Hiram's lower eyelid.

Hiram scrunched his eyes shut, knowing that it would do nothing to protect his eye. His heart roared in his ears. It hurt, but it wasn't the pain. It was the ungodly horror of that knife in his eye, the jelly of it dripping down his cheek, the knife sliding through the socket to his brain.

Blackwell pressed a little harder, drawing blood.

Hiram whispered, "It's in the middle, page four thirty-something, I don't know exactly."

The other mage drew back. "Which book?"

"The second one," he said, feeling sick to his stomach.

Blackwell set the knife aside and took up the second book. He leafed through it for a while and finally looked up. "I knew you could be reasonable," he said.

He took the book and walked away, leaving Hiram in the chair.

Sniffling, blood and tears on his cheeks, Hiram worked at the ropes that tied him, as he did every time he was left alone; he did nothing more than tip his chair over, setting his wounds throbbing.

Blackwell returned minutes later, glanced at Hiram on the floor and gestured for Eddie to right him.

"Move him and the table out of the way," the mage instructed, "We'll need the room."

Eddie moved them both to the side, being gentle with Hiram.

"I'm sorry," Hiram whispered.

"There's nothing to be sorry for, you've saved me several

days at least," Blackwell said.

"He's bleeding a lot, Mr. Blackwell," Eddie said, "You think I should clean him up?"

"Oh, no use, he'll be dead…" Blackwell trailed off. He turned to look at Hiram. "What script is this spell written in? The runes…this is definitely not standard. You can read this?"

"It's Germanic long-form," Hiram said.

Blackwell made a face. "All the long-form scripts went out of style centuries ago."

"They're more precise," Hiram said, "This sort of magic needs precision."

"And the instructions…they're not even in English, are they? The words stutter on the page. Been giving me a frightful headache."

"Old Saxon," Hiram admitted, "My father and I spent…seven years working that translation."

"Clever, though, laying a spell over…" Blackwell mused, clearly distracted. "What are you doing enchanting trinkets and working harvest spells if *this* is the sort of thing of which you're capable?"

"Making a living."

Blackwell laughed heartily, then turned back to the book. While he traced the summoning circle and aligned the objects within it, Hiram slipped one hand out of his bonds. He reached for the knife on the table, but Blackwell plucked it out of his reach and said, "Now, I'll need you to read this gibberish for me. Germanic long-form *script*, what nonsense."

Hiram shook his head.

"Come now, we both know I've found your breaking point, or should I jab a bigger hole in your eye?"

"You haven't got to kill anyone. Your wife isn't even dead!"

"It would be better for her if she was," Blackwell said and set the point of the knife against Hiram's other eye.

He held out the book before him.

Hiram swallowed, then began to read, praying that he would be able to set this right in some way, that he wasn't condemning Phaedrus and Blackwell's wife to a horrible death.

Blackwell withdrew the knife and took the book back when Hiram completed the chant. He stared at the summoning circle. "It didn't work."

"It takes time," Hiram said, "It says so in the spells preface. Otherwise, it'd be pieces, not a person."

Blackwell glanced at him. "I'm starting to dislike you. Here I was a minute ago thinking I'd keep you around to read these spells for me, but I'd rather slog through with a dictionary."

Hiram didn't tell him that the only Germanic long-form script dictionaries left in the world were in royal and university libraries of Triviai or the personal possession of the Reinhart family.

Phaedrus appeared in the circle; they looked around, bewildered, and at the same time closing their robe around their body, covering the thin silk shirt against their skin. Moon-pale eyes ringed in black searched the room, first lighting on Hiram, then Blackwell.

"I'm sorry," Hiram said.

"My goodness, your eye...You look terrible," Phaedrus said. They turned their eyes to Blackwell. "All this over a woman who wanted to be away from you? For shame."

"I'll get her back."

Phaedrus shook their head. "No."

"That's what he said, too," Blackwell said, nodding towards Hiram.

"There's nothing you can do to me while I am within this circle," Phaedrus reminded placidly, "And if you let me out, the advantage will be mine."

"Yes, yes," Blackwell drawled. He took from the table a cuff similar to the one around Hiram's wrist and approached the circle. "Eddie."

Eddie came forward, and when Blackwell scuffed the chalk circle with his toe, Eddie grabbed Phaedrus' arm and yanked them forward; Blackwell slipped the cuff around their wrist. It took no more than half a minute.

"In the chair," Blackwell said.

"We haven't got another chair," Eddie said, glancing at Hiram.

"Fine, put it in the cell and—"

"It's very near to three, sir," Eddie said. "Perhaps you'd do better starting this another time."

"Oh, the De Launciers, of course! Put them both in the cell and then ready the carriage. I've got to change," Blackwell said and walked out.

"The De Launciers?" Hiram asked, recognizing the name of the family.

"He hopes to snag the oldest daughter for his next wife. Of course, before Mrs. Blackwell went, he hoped to have her for a mistress, so not much has changed," Eddie said. He took Phaedrus over to the cell.

He closed them in and went over for Hiram. "I've got to get his things ready, but I'll be back down to check on you."

"Thank you, Eddie," Hiram said, sagging heavily against him. His legs had gone numb from so many hours tied to the chair.

He curled up on the floor of the closet and heard Eddie leaving. He heard Phaedrus checking the door, shaking the lock and trying a few spells but getting no results. He sat up after half a minute or so, noticing a faint, silver light that hadn't ever been there before.

"Your eyes," Hiram said.

"What? Oh, of course," Phaedrus said, "The light, I forget sometimes." The creature crouched beside him, examining him. "You look a fright. How long has he had you?"

"What day is it?"

"August seventh."

Hiram, at first, felt numb, but then began to laugh; he couldn't stop, not even when he began to ache.

"What is it?" they asked.

"It's my birthday," he gasped.

"Oh."

"I'm twenty-six," he said. The mania that had caused his laughter faded, replaced with the idea that he would never see twenty-seven.

A quiet settled between the two of them, heavy and anxious.

"I never got your name, when you came to warn me with that inquisitive friend of yours," the demon said.

"Hiram Montgomery Reinhart," he said, "Of the Georgia branch, though now of Canada."

"Reinhart? Not the same family that took...well, I suppose it would be rude to ask."

"The family that had June, yes," Hiram said.

"But Junius is free now, isn't he? That's what people have said. I've heard his story second-hand."

"Yes. He's free."

"Hmm," they said and looked at Hiram for a little while. "I think your nose is broken."

"It feels broken."

"Would you like me to set it? Or would you prefer to leave it crooked?" Phaedrus asked.

"Um...I suppose it would be best to put it back," the mage admitted.

They reached out, the sleeves of their robe brushing his face, and pushed his nose back into place.

Hiram did not shout or scream, as it was a small pain compared to what he had felt recently, but he did grit his teeth and grunt.

The creature took their hands back and Hiram reached up gingerly to touch his nose.

The two of them sat in silence again with Phaedrus looking down at their hair, their eyes illuminating locks the color of a fawn's coat, until Hiram asked, "So...if you don't mind me asking, what type are you?"

Stiffly, Phaedrus answered, "I believe I've answered that already."

"Oh...I, no, I'm sorry," Hiram said. "I meant what sort of angel were you?"

Sheepishly, they answered, "I'm a storyteller. I know the myths, the legends, I collect the lore. I tell you this with the caveat that I know what is said, not what is true. For example, I know what is said about Queen Eleanor I and her violinist, but not what truly transpired between them."

"Have you got claws?"

"Pardon?"

"June has claws."

"No, I haven't," Phaedrus said.

"Oh. I didn't really expect that you would."

"You sound disappointed."

Hiram shook his head. "No, why would I be?"

He had hoped that maybe the demon would have claws because he had the suspicion that if he could wedge something into the seam on his cuff, he would be able to get it off, but it was only a suspicion. He would ask Eddie for something.

"You say he plans to kill me," came Phaedrus' voice.

"After he gets his wife back."

Phaedrus sighed. "And he will get her back, I'm afraid," they said. "I don't do well with torture."

"Neither do I, it seems," Hiram said.

"You haven't got a plan?"

"Eddie's helping me with what he can. Can you see in the dark?"

"A little bit," Phaedrus said, "But that's a trait among my kind. It hasn't got anything to do with my eyes...well, the glowing, anyway. It's decorative."

"Oh."

Hiram moved aside his blanket and pillow to find the candles and matches that Eddie had snuck him. He lit one and held out his hand to Phaedrus. "I'd like to take a look at yours, too."

Phaedrus gave him their hand. "You don't think they're the same?"

"If I were the one making these, I'd make them different for mages and creatures, but maybe Eddie didn't know to get something different for you," Hiram said, holding their hand in one of his and running the fingers of his other over the cuff, peering at the runes.

He tried not to think about the pleasant weight and warmth of their hand and did not allow himself to get sidetracked by imagining what would happen if he put their hand against his cheek. If he touched his lips to their knuckles.

"Is it different?" Phaedrus asked.

"There are variations, yes, though nothing specific to the type of creature that you are. It's for things that are magical and not human," he said. "It could be helpful, or it could be useless."

"May I have my hand back?" they asked after a moment.

"My apologies," Hiram said and released them.

Neither said anything more for a while.

EDDIE CAME about an hour later and allowed them out of the cell. He brought food and medical items. Hiram elected to eat first, though Phaedrus declined to eat at all. Eddie cleaned Hiram's wounds as best he could, frowning the whole time.

"If you want her to live, you'll let us go," Phaedrus said to Eddie as he gathered up his things to leave.

"If I let you go, he'll kill me," Eddie said, "And he'll find you again."

"And what of the child?" they asked.

Eddie swallowed hard.

"Can I have a knife?" Hiram asked.

Eddie gestured towards the one on the table; he didn't leave and seemed to be waiting for something.

Hiram went and took up the knife, sliding the tip along the seam of the cuff. He thought he would be able to work it through and break the bond; he'd need to be careful, or he'd open a vein.

"The child," Phaedrus reminded.

"I know!" Eddie shouted. "But if I let you go, he'll find you in a heartbeat."

Phaedrus said nothing more, only looked at Eddie, who

turned his eyes away and took his supplies with him. He had left his lantern.

Hiram wondered if he would ever see daylight again.

"Enjoy the space while you can," Hiram advised. "He'll put us back in a little while."

The creature paced, trying the door, pawing through the scraps that Eddie had left behind, examining every inch of the room.

"Don't you think I've tried to get out?" Hiram asked.

They frowned at him. "I've got to try."

Hiram thought about arguing but didn't know what he would say; there was no argument against trying to escape. He sat on the bench and pressed the tip of the knife into the seam; he pressed too hard, sending the point skittering down the cuff and into his palm.

He recoiled, dropping the knife and shouting.

"You really believe that you can get that off?" they asked.

"I've got to try," he said.

Phaedrus sat beside him on the bench, a small smile on their lips. "I don't mean to come across as unpleasant, but fear brings out the worst in me."

Hiram looked up. "No, I...I understand. I'm not exactly at my best either. And it's my fault we're here, in any case."

"I doubt that's all there is to it," Phaedrus said. "If I had not helped his wife, if you had not done whatever it is that you did, things would be different, but in the end, it's not you or I that's out for blood."

Hiram looked down at his hand, watching the blood dribbling out. It wasn't a bad cut and would scab over soon. "I read for him. I told him on which page he would find the spell," he confessed.

"Under a great deal of duress, I imagine," Phaedrus said.

"Still...if I hadn't...he wouldn't have been able to read the spell. He would have had to give up or delay for months, at least."

"Don't blame yourself too much, Hiram," the creature said. "I can call you Hiram, can't I? Or should it still be Mr.

Reinhart?"

"Hiram is fine."

"I'd hoped so," they said. "These do seem to be informal circumstances."

Eddie returned and took them individually upstairs to wash and relieve themselves; Hiram scrubbed as best he could, hoping to look a little more presentable, though he could do nothing about the scabs, burns, and bruises or the stains on his clothes. It was a foolish desire, he knew, considering the circumstances, but he always tried to look fit to be seen.

After that, Eddie ushered them to the closet, saying, "Blackwell will be home soon."

"You can still release us," Phaedrus reminded him.

"I'd prefer it if you could escape," Eddie said, which Hiram thought was fair enough. The answer did not please Phaedrus, though, because they crossed their arms and sniffed.

Once the door closed, Hiram heard Phaedrus sigh and knew that they must have closed their eyes because the timid light had disappeared.

"Have you still got that knife, Hiram?"

"Yes."

"Kill me," they said, their voice flat.

"See, that's the original issue. Killing things doesn't sit well with me," Hiram said. "Besides, you can't mean that."

"Why can't I?"

"You seem the sort of person that likes being alive."

"I do?" they asked. "Why?"

"You dress in fine clothes, you have pearls at your throat, and you smell of violets and honey," Hiram said, "A person who didn't like to be alive wouldn't care for themself so."

"Maybe finery is my last refuge in this bleak world," Phaedrus said.

Hiram said, "I don't think so. Violets are romantic, not morbid."

"You've caught me, Hiram. I am romantic, not morbid," they said and opened their eyes, a little bit of light touching their face. "So what will we do?"

"I don't know when he'll come back for you, but try to last. If I can get this cuff off, then we can escape."

"I don't know if I can. Torture sits poorly with me."

Hiram thought that torture sat badly with everyone, but it felt rude, so he took out a candle and once it was lit, he began again to work at the seam.

"Is there anyone who might be looking for you?" Hiram asked.

"No."

They returned to quiet.

"Are you the one that set him free?" Phaedrus asked.

"Who?" Hiram asked, not paying attention. He had made a lot of scratches, which gave him hope.

"When I heard the story that June tells, he said that a young man set him free, but he didn't give a name. But if your family was the one that had him, it makes sense," Phaedrus said. "He's sparse on a lot of the details, though. I don't blame him."

Hiram said nothing.

"But was it you?"

"Yes," the mage admitted.

"Why?" Phaedrus asked. "Out of the goodness of your heart?"

Hiram scowled and let out a breath through his nose.

"You must have a lot of goodness in there if you went through this for a stranger," the creature said.

Hiram knew that they were looking at him. "No. It was selfish."

"Oh?"

His father had railed for days after Hiram had released June. He had never understood why Hiram had cared about June. Hiram had never had the guts to explain it. Not to his father, not to anyone. He'd only ever spoken about such feelings with June. Phaedrus didn't seem the sort to judge, though, and even if they were, they'd both likely be dead soon. "I had feelings for him. I thought that if I helped him, he would love me, too."

"But he left."

"Of course he left," Hiram said.

"Can I have that pillow?" the creature asked.

Hiram put aside the knife for a moment to pass it.

They arranged themself more comfortably so that they lay on their side.

Hiram returned to his work with the knife, and they both remained quiet for a while.

"Would you like to hear a story? I have a lot of them."

Hiram paused and looked at them. "If you want to tell one."

"What kind of story do you like? I like love stories," they said.

"So then tell me one of those," Hiram said, "if that's what you prefer."

"But what do you prefer? I know all my stories already."

The mage paused and looked at the creature, wishing he could see their face by something more than candlelight. "Tell me your favorite story."

Phaedrus smiled. "In Connemara, long ago, there was a fisherman's wife, and he was always lucky so that she had fish at all times to sell in the market. But at night a cat would come and devour up all her fish so that she came to keep a great stick by her side. And here's an author's note, Hiram, the story's going to say that it's a black cat, but I tell you, a black cat is never the Devil. So can we pretend that the story says it's gray, or are you a traditionalist?"

"It can be a gray cat, certainly," he said.

"Wonderful," Phaedrus said, smiling. "One day, as she and another woman were carding together, the house got dark and..." They trailed off as they heard a commotion.

Hiram blew out the candle, hiding it and the knife under the blanket. A hand found his in the darkness and he gripped it tight.

The door opened and Phaedrus recoiled.

"I need...that one," Eddie said, clearly unsure how to address Phaedrus, whose facial features and body shape did not strictly evoke those of a woman, while their dress and mannerisms had enough feminine traits to never be mistaken for a man's.

Hiram squeezed their hand one more time and said, "Last as long as you can."

Phaedrus nodded, then released Hiram's hand and stood, clenching their robe in their fists in an attempt to hide the trembling.

Eddie closed the door on him.

Hiram took up the knife, determined to remove the cuff, wondering if a better solution would be to remove the hand entirely. Missing a hand might be a hindrance to his spell casting, and he did not want to lose it, but he did not want to die in this place either.

He continued to work at the cuff, moving closer to the door and listening. He heard Blackwell make his usual pleasant appeal for cooperation and Phaedrus' refusal. Hiram winced at the creature's cry.

"The house got dark and the door burst open," he heard their voice, "And a great gray cat walked in, right up to the fire, then turned and growled at them."

"Stop blithering," Blackwell said.

"A girl who was sorting fish nearby said, 'Surely it's the Devil,' and the cat said, 'I'll show you how to call names' and jumped up, scratching her arm until she bled."

For the better part of an hour, Blackwell demanded to know where his wife was and got nothing out of Phaedrus but screams and Irish folktales. He gave up, claiming boredom and promising the creature that they would give up their secret soon enough.

Eddie returned them to the closet, setting them on the floor.

Hiram grabbed his trouser leg before he left. "Can you get me a saw or a hatchet?" he whispered.

Eddie ignored him, but Hiram felt confident that he had heard.

Hiram took the pillow and scooted over to the creature,

saying "Lift your head."

"I can't."

"I'm sure you can and that you're being dramatic."

Phaedrus opened their eyes to glare at him.

Hiram pushed the pillow towards their face. "Lift your head." This time the creature lifted their head and Hiram tucked the pillow under them. "I knew you had it in you."

"I won't make it if he goes at me again." They closed their eyes again and settled into the pillow.

"You thought you wouldn't make it through this," Hiram reasoned. "I have a plan, though, one I know will work if Eddie gets me what I need."

Phaedrus nodded.

"I liked the stories you told," Hiram said. "Are you cold?"

"A little."

Hiram took the blanket and tucked it around them. "You'll need to eat when Eddie brings food."

"Any luck getting that thing off?"

"A little," he lied. He had done nothing more than hurt himself and mar the surface.

"Good."

Eddie brought them both food that night and they ate together quietly. The young man had not brought the other things for which Hiram had asked, but he had not expected results so soon.

"In the morning, he'll be back," Eddie said when he took their plates. "Try to sleep."

Neither of them slept well, and finally Hiram, after lying awake for what felt like hours, asked, "Phaedrus?"

"Yes?"

"Are you asleep?"

"No."

"I can't sleep either," Hiram said.

"Not used to sleeping alone?" Phaedrus asked.

"I've never done anything but sleep alone," Hiram admitted.

"Really? I thought you and that Julian fellow were

involved...you blushed terribly when he asked what I was. I thought it had to be jealousy."

"No. He has a fiancée."

"Sorry. I assumed."

Hiram said nothing.

"You've really never...?" Phaedrus asked, "No, don't answer. I'm being rude again."

Hiram remained quiet.

"Unless you want to answer."

Hiram chuckled. "No, I've never. I've never anything with anyone."

"Never?"

"Ever."

The creature said, "But you wanted to. With June."

"With several men," Hiram said, "But nothing has ever come of it."

"Why not? There doesn't seem to be anything wrong with you."

"Depends on who you ask," the mage said. He waited a little while. "What about you?"

"What about me?"

"Do, uh...do you sleep alone?" Hiram asked, feeling their eyes on him and wondering if they could see him blush.

"As a rule, I avoid intimate entanglements," Phaedrus said.

Hiram pushed himself up a little. "That's got to be a lie. You said you were romantic."

"I am."

"But you avoid romance?"

"Yes."

"Why?"

"It's a very maudlin answer, I'm afraid."

Hiram lay back down, turning so he faced towards Phaedrus. "Tell me anyway."

"The people that are interested in me, they're interested for a singular reason. They want a man that looks like a woman or a woman that looks like a man, something exotic to play with for a night or two," Phaedrus said. "Or maybe they get me undressed and are alarmed to find that I am not what they expected. Wrong body parts. That tends to upset people."

"Oh."

"It's *not* romantic," the demon said. "And I can't bear any more disappointment."

Hiram didn't know what to say but felt a powerful need to offer comfort, so he reached out and put his hand on Phaedrus' arm. "There doesn't seem to be anything wrong with you either. I'm sure you'll find someone."

"I'm sure you will too," they said, putting their hand on his. "If we get out of here."

"We will," Hiram assured, closing his eyes and knowing when they had closed theirs because that small silver light disappeared.

ANOTHER DAY passed, and Eddie still did not produce either of the things Hiram had requested. The young man had left the door open, which Hiram wasn't sure if he appreciated, not enjoying the clearer sounds of Phaedrus being tortured.

Hiram pushed the closet door open.

Blackwell paused his work, looking up. "Mr. Reinhart, is there something I can do for you?"

"Leave Phaedrus alone, leave your wife alone. Let me go home," Hiram said.

"I'm afraid that's not possible," Blackwell said and, with a chant and a gesture, sent Hiram toppling.

"Don't," Phaedrus said.

"Don't?" Blackwell asked. "Nothing but nonsense fairy stories and finally I get a protest?"

Hiram did not like the curious tone in his voice. He liked it even less when Blackwell came over to him, seized him by the arm, and dragged him toward Phaedrus.

The older man said, "Maybe leaving you down here wasn't an oversight. It seems the creature and you have bonded. You did always sound overly fond of foul things."

Phaedrus stared down Blackwell. "Leave him. He doesn't

know anything," they insisted.

Blackwell took up a knife and pressed it into Hiram's neck, right beneath his ear. "Tell me where she is, or I'll paint you with his blood."

Phaedrus fixed their eyes on Hiram's.

"Don't," Hiram said. "It's not worth it."

Blackwell poked the knife in a little bit, sending a shock of pain through him and a gout of blood down his neck. Hiram grunted, and he could see that this might be too much for the creature. It was one thing, Hiram knew, to put others above yourself, but he didn't know how quickly he would have given in if Blackwell had made him responsible for another's suffering.

He looked at the table, his eyes scanning the items he had brought with which to torture them. Among those items lay a hatchet, and he knew why Eddie had left the door open that day. He bit Blackwell and lunged for the hatchet.

Blackwell began to chant.

Hiram slammed the blade of the hatchet into his arm, about an inch above the cuff.

The spell he had meant to say came out as a bellow, but he didn't mangle the words and it sent Blackwell flying backward.

He smacked into the wall and crumbled to the floor, limp.

Hiram took one more step, hesitated, feeling woozy. He dropped to his knees, but it put him right before Phaedrus. With his remaining hand, he reached for the demon's bonds.

The door crashed open and Eddie entered.

"Please."

"I can't let you go, you'll have to stop me," Eddie said.

"Will you untie them first?" Hiram asked.

"Stop his bleeding!" Phaedrus insisted.

Eddie took a piece of rope and tied it around Hiram's arm. "He needs a doctor."

"Untie," Hiram said.

Eddie untied Phaedrus, and once free, the first thing the

creature did was remove the rope from Hiram's arm and replaced it with a pad of cloth made from a sleeve ripped from his robe. They pressed the pad to the stump and wound fabric from the other sleeve to secure it. They took what was left of their robe and wrapped it around Hiram.

They did all this with speed and certainty and shortly after, wrapped a bruised and burnt arm around Hiram and lifted him, holding him close.

"I *can't* let you go," Eddie said, grabbing Phaedrus' arm.

Hiram put his hand on the young man's chest and muttered a spell.

Eddie crumpled to the floor.

"We should kill him," Phaedrus said, glancing at Blackwell.

"I know. But I don't like killing things."

"No, me neither," the demon agreed and tightened their grip on Hiram, half-carrying him through the door and up the stairs. "Do you know where we are?"

Hiram shook his head and did his best to walk on his own. They exited the house together and found a carriage and driver in front of the house.

"Are you the ones I'm waiting for?" the driver, another young man with dark skin, asked.

"Eddie sent us," Phaedrus said.

"Get in," the driver said.

The demon helped Hiram into the carriage and said, "We need to go to a doctor. Of the magical variety, if possible."

"I'll get you to what's closest," the driver said.

Phaedrus didn't argue, and neither did Hiram. "They look remarkably similar," Phaedrus observed. "I'd say brothers."

Hiram grunted. He didn't care if Eddie had a brother or not. The ride to the doctor took longer than he could bear. He lost consciousness several times, but each time Phaedrus woke him back up, pleading with him to stay awake.

He had to be carried into the doctor's home, and the old man ogled Phaedrus for a while before he began to attend to

Hiram's wound. The doctor's first step was to shove something into Hiram's mouth to bite down on, but he passed out before the surgery was finished.

He woke up with a clean, white bandage wound around his stump and treatments applied to the rest of his wounds.

He sat up.

Phaedrus said, "Lie back down."

"My arm is shorter than it was."

"He had to take a little more off...the bone was too sharp..."

Hiram nodded. "I hate to say this—"

"Whatever it is, don't," the demon warned.

"I have to go back. He has my books, and he can summon you again, bind another of the Fallen to his will with them. Not to mention Eddie...leaving him in such a predicament would be immoral."

"I can't..."

Hiram said, "I'm not asking you to go with me."

"You can't go alone."

Hiram sat up and looked at Phaedrus for a while, taking in the blood that had crusted in their hair and on their pearls, the wounds that blemished the jade of their skin. Their arms were bare, their robe discarded as rags now, leaving them in only loose-fitting silk trousers with cinched ankles and a thin silk shirt with no sleeves and the collarless neckline unlaced.

"You're staring," they said.

Hiram shook his head. "I don't mean to be rude."

"But you are being rude," Phaedrus said. "Staring is as bad as asking."

"No, I..."

Phaedrus stood and walked away. They snatched a blanket and wrapped it around their shoulders, hiding what had been revealed. They did not return to Hiram's bedside.

Hiram swung his legs out of bed but paused when he realized most of his clothing had been removed.

"Please come back," he called.

"So you can stare at me some more?" they accused.

"Phaedrus, please," he said. "I'm sorry, and I won't any longer."

They glanced back. "Don't go back there."

"Blackwell isn't dead, and he won't stop at this. You don't hold people captive and then just let them get away. It's not finished."

"I know!"

Hiram sighed. "Will you find me something to wear, at least? I'll speak to Julian. Perhaps he'll be able to assist me."

Phaedrus said nothing, their fingers working at something on their wrist before Hiram remembered that their cuff had not been removed.

"I know where to go to get that off," he offered.

"So do I," the creature said.

The doctor came in. "Oh, your color is much better now."

"Sir, could I trouble you for something to wear? You can add it to my bill, of course," Hiram said, wondering how he would be able to pay this bill.

"Yes, yes, but let me take a look at you first. I'm not sending you out half put back together," he said and glanced at Phaedrus, then added, "Maybe you'll want to give the gentleman some privacy."

Phaedrus shed the blanket and left. "Don't worry about the clothes," they said on their way out. "I'll be back."

AT FIRST, Hiram believed that Phaedrus would return, but when hours had passed and the creature remained away, he began to worry. While he waited, he washed and ate; he borrowed a dressing robe from the doctor and knocked things over a few times when he tried to grab them with a hand that wasn't there.

"Young man, you're very welcome to stay the night if you need to," the doctor's wife told him as evening drew to a close and night began.

"It won't be necessary," the doctor said, "That strange-looking one has returned."

Phaedrus entered the house without knocking, smelling again of violets and honey, their hair and skin free of crusted blood. They wore a loose tunic belted at the waist and draped trousers, all dark gray and made of something sturdier than silk.

They handed Hiram a change of clothes more typical of modern dress. "It took longer than expected to have that thing removed and to settle affairs at the boarding house. My rent was overdue."

"Of course," Hiram said.

Phaedrus left him alone to change, and when he emerged, he found them settling his doctor's bill.

"Oh, you can't..."

"Don't tell me what I can't do," they said. "Are you ready to go?"

"Yes."

"Good," they said and turned away.

Hiram hurried after them, rushing out the door. "Wait."

"Why? I need to go somewhere safe."

"There is nowhere safe," Hiram said. "The summoning will reach you anywhere."

"The town is lousy with mages, I'm sure one can counteract the spell," they said, still walking away. The driver who had brought them had left long ago, perhaps returning to Blackwell, if he was bound in the same way Eddie was.

Hiram hurried as well as he could to catch up with the creature, who seemed to intend to leave him behind. Hiram reached out and grabbed them by the sleeve, his fingers barely grasping it. "You're walking away from a mage that can. No one else knows those books."

"Let me go," Phaedrus said.

Hiram released them immediately. "What's upsetting you?"

"A man wants me *dead* and he's already captured me once. I will give up that woman's location, and she will die, and I will die."

Hiram sighed. "I want to prevent that, Phaedrus. I thought my intention was clear."

"It is."

"Then why are you angry with me?" Hiram asked. "I don't understand."

"Do what you need to do. You don't need my help. I'm going back to my life. Spending a few days held captive together doesn't make us friends," Phaedrus said.

Hiram didn't know what to say. When Phaedrus walked away again, he didn't follow or call after them. His first thought was to go home, but he remembered that Eddie had found him there easily last time.

Julian's home would be an obvious target as well. He had no money on him and wouldn't be able to rent a room or even buy a meal. He resigned himself to preying on Julian's hospitality, and when he knocked on the door, Julian's sister gasped and called for her brother to come immediately.

Julian rushed into the room and embraced Hiram. "God, we all thought you were dead."

"Blackwell had me," he said.

"No, we went to his house! Three times. We searched the whole thing."

"He has a basement."

"A basement! We didn't find one...oh, Hiram, I feel horrible!" Julian embraced him again.

Hiram hugged him back, allowing himself this comfort, though it meant more to him than it did to Julian.

After a moment, the other mage pulled back and looked him over, then did a double-take. "What's happened to your hand?"

Hiram glanced down. "It's gone."

"How?" he demanded.

"I had to escape. I cut it off," he said. "Listen, I need to get back there. He has my books, and his mission isn't finished."

"Not now, Hiram. That's madness."

"No, but soon," Hiram said. "A few days of rest and then...I'd appreciate your help in the matter."

"Of course."

"Don't tell anyone I'm here."

"No, I wouldn't."

"Would you mind terribly if I retired?" Hiram asked. He realized he hadn't even asked permission to stay. "My house...I don't think it's safe to return..."

"No, of course not," Julian said, taking Hiram by the arm and walking him upstairs. "In the morning, you'll have to fill me in more."

"In the morning," Hiram agreed.

He slept restlessly but stayed in bed late into the morning. Julian checked in on him and asked if he was ready to talk. Hiram was not ready to talk, but he did it anyway, sparsely relating the tale, not wanting to repeat many of the details.

At the end of the story, Julian rubbed the back of his neck and said, "I think...maybe more than a few days of rest would do you well. If he can't read the script, it will take him time to accomplish anything on his own."

"I wouldn't want anything else to go wrong," Hiram said. He thought for a moment, then asked, "Would you mind if I wrote a letter? I'd like to assure my family that—"

"That things are well? They aren't."

"That they are safe and to stay where they are," he said, thinking that they might have started to worry, not necessarily at the length of their holiday to the country, but at his lack of contact.

"I'll bring you stationary. As long as that isn't your writing hand."

Hiram thought for a moment, then shook his head. "No, it isn't."

After eating and writing the letter, he returned to bed, lacking the motivation to do anything else. At first, he couldn't sleep, too bothered by what Phaedrus had said and worried that Blackwell would find him again.

HIRAM SLEPT on and off for several days until he grew restless and petulant. He wandered around Julian's home with no goal and nothing to occupy him. Julian asked him if he was feeling well, and he answered truthfully, "No. I feel terrible."

"The hand?"

Hiram glanced at his hand. "No, it's not that. It's…"

"Phaedrus?"

His face grew hot.

"I had my suspicions, I must admit," Julian said.

"I don't know what I did to make them so angry with me."

"It can be a little thing, you know. It doesn't have to be something large."

"But to say that we aren't friends?" Hiram said, "I mean…we didn't get along badly while we were together."

"Hiram, Blackwell had you much longer than he had the creature, and that whole time, who were you trying to protect?" Julian asked.

"You think I'm foolish, don't you?'

"No, I think you're sentimental. It isn't a bad thing."

Hiram nodded.

"Bathe, get dressed, eat something. You'll feel better," he said. "I'll be back in a little while."

"You're going out?"

"I'm trying to get something that will be useful for our venture," Julian replied and headed out.

Hiram did as Julian suggested and felt a little better once he was clean and fed.

Julian returned and called into the house, "Hiram? Are you decent?"

"Yes," he called back. "I'm in the parlor."

Julian entered the parlor and said, "I've brought someone."

Hiram looked up to see that Julian was accompanied by a displeased-looking Phaedrus. "Oh," he said. He glanced at Julian and asked, "You didn't make them come, did you?"

"He didn't," Phaedrus said. "He was only irritatingly insistent. Something about you being in a terrible melancholy."

"Julian," Hiram sighed.

"I said it might have more to do with being held captive by a murderous lunatic and cutting off your own hand," Phaedrus said.

Hiram glanced at Julian, who had started to back out of the room. "Where are you going?" Hiram asked.

"Talk to each other, please. I won't go into this without you having a clear head," Julian said, closing the door behind him as he left.

Phaedrus crossed their arms.

"I'm not melancholy," Hiram said.

"No?" the creature asked. "Then why has your friend dragged me here, saying that you are?"

Hiram rubbed his eyes. "We aren't friends. You said it yourself. You don't need to concern yourself with my affairs any longer."

"No, but my safety depends on your getting your books back or ending Blackwell. The longer you wait, the more danger I'm in."

"I know."

The creature said nothing; they wandered the parlor, touching a few things, then glancing over at Hiram, who had stood and taken a single step towards them. "Tell me this mood is to do with your hand and not with me."

Hiram let out a small laugh. "I have to say, I don't miss the hand very much. It's inconvenient, but...I think I'll be all right without it. It's an odd feeling."

Phaedrus waited.

"It was only a few days, I know," he said, "But...I don't know. I don't. I had the hand my whole life, and I miss it less than I miss you."

"You like men," the demon said.

"Yes."

"I am not a man."

Hiram took another half step, then pulled back. "I don't expect you to be."

"Everyone expects me to be something I'm not," Phaedrus said. "I'm done being a curiosity. Done."

"I...that's not how I think of you."

"You stared," they accused. "You're staring now."

"I can't help it."

The creature shook their head. "That doesn't make it acceptable. You decided that you have the right to examine me—"

"And do you know what I've noticed?" Hiram asked, appalled at himself for interrupting.

"I don't care!"

"You have a scar on your jaw, and it runs up to almost touch your bottom lip, so faint it must be older than I am. One of your teeth is chipped— the corner is missing. You have a callus on your index finger on your right hand, from holding your pen too tightly, I'd be willing to bet, because I have the same thing," Hiram said. "And you have freckles, just a handful, right over your nose and cheeks."

Phaedrus blinked at him and licked their lips.

Hiram swallowed.

"And if you undressed me, do you know what you'd notice?" they asked.

"That you have more freckles?" Hiram dared to joke, his mouth turning up at one corner.

Phaedrus didn't smile, not even a little. "You'll see what everyone else sees," they said. "Dressed, with jewelry and cosmetics, with perfume and hair combs, I can be something else, something beyond labels and definitions. People see what I want. Without those things, people see something they can label, body parts they can categorize. You will think of me as something I'm not."

"So then tell me we can't be lovers," Hiram said, "but don't tell me we can't be friends."

Phaedrus wiped one eye with their sleeve and said, "Christ, you actually mean that, don't you?"

"Yes."

"Come here," they said.

Hiram obeyed, meeting them halfway as they crossed the parlor.

The creature embraced him, burying their face in his neck. "If we make it out of this alive, we will see what we can be."

Hiram tightened his arms around them, closing his eyes, glad for the feel of another's skin against his. "You don't need to come with us."

"I'm much older than you. Don't you think I might know a few useful things?"

"There is that."

Smiling, they pulled back and said, "Yes, of course, there is that."

Someone knocked on the parlor door. "Hiram?" Julian asked.

"Come in."

The man entered. "You look much happier. Are things resolved between you two?"

They both nodded, and Hiram said, "Yes, I believe so."

"Good. Let's get those books back before anything else

happens. You've only got one hand left, you know," he said and walked away.

Hiram followed him out. "But I've got two feet."

Julian laughed, and Phaedrus shook their head.

Together they walked to Blackwell's house and hesitated before the door, exchanging looks. Julian tried the knob and found it unlocked.

"Do you think he's waiting for us?" Hiram asked softly.

"Almost certainly," Julian said, "You are vocal about your fondness for those books."

"They are *mine*," Hiram said.

"Knowing what they say about your family, I shudder to think what other spells are in there," Phaedrus said.

Hiram glanced at them. "What do they say about my family?" he asked.

"By the worry in your tone, you already know what they say," the demon replied.

"I've never heard anything about your family," Julian said. "You're the only Reinhart I've ever met."

"It is better that way," Phaedrus assured him and pushed in front of the other two, stepping through the door. "Oh."

"Oh?" Hiram asked.

"Oh dear," Phaedrus said.

Hiram and Julian joined them inside.

Hiram put a hand to his heart. "Oh, the poor soul..." he said, unable to look away from Eddie's body. A dark splotch of blood stained his shirt in the place where Hiram recalled there being a piece of glass.

He approached and peered inside the shirt, then recoiled. The glass had been removed, leaving the flesh ragged and a hole in his chest the size of a fist. He examined Eddie's body more closely and saw that the young man bore wounds similar to the ones that he and Phaedrus wore.

"Eddie...he did not happen to know where you brought Mrs. Blackwell, did he?" Hiram asked, looking at the demon, whose eyes were trained on Eddie's face.

"I advised her not to tell anyone, but the secrets that are

shared between lovers..." Phaedrus began, reaching out a hand to touch Eddie's face. They paused, stepped back, and cleared their throat. "It is possible she might have told him. Or even been foolish enough to send him a message. I hope not. Blackwell may have simply blamed the young man for our escape."

They all stood and looked at the body; seconds ticked past, feeling like minutes, and Hiram's ears filled up with a vast, buzzing silence. He had the feeling that something was wrong. "We should check for the books," he said, heading towards the basement.

The other two joined him to search and Julian exclaimed, "My God! Hiram, is that your blood?"

Hiram glanced at the stain. "Yes."

Julian shuddered. "What happened to your hand? I mean to ask, did you take it when you left?"

"No."

"I don't see it," Julian said.

"Wonderful, let's not dwell on it."

They found neither the books nor Hiram's hand in the basement. They returned upstairs and searched all the rooms for several hours, jumpy and never raising their voices above a whisper. They didn't find Hiram's books, but they also didn't come across Blackwell, which proved to be a relief.

Before they left, Hiram looked at Eddie's body and Phaedrus said, "You're right, we ought to do something about him. We can't leave him here."

"What do you think he did with your hand?" Julian asked.

"I hope he did something sensible and threw it away," Hiram said.

"I'll be right back," Phaedrus said and left the house.

Hiram trailed after him and watched from the door as the creature walked up the street, delicately stepping around puddles from last night's rain, and knocked on the door of Blackwell's neighbor.

An older black woman wearing a servant's uniform

answered the door; Hiram could not hear what they discussed, but they spoke for several minutes. Phaedrus nodded a lot, gave a very small bow, and the woman returned inside. The creature made their way back towards Blackwell's and said, "She says that Blackwell left days ago with a new driver and hasn't been back. No one else has been by the house."

"A new driver?"

"I'm sure he met a similar fate as the other young man," Phaedrus said. "But no one else has been by."

"So?" Julian asked.

"So no one is looking for him," Phaedrus said.

"He always had some appointment or other," Hiram said.

"So he's in town keeping his appointments," Julian said, "Or he's told people he's going away."

"But what are we going to do about Eddie's body?" the demon asked.

Julian looked at Hiram. "Should we tell the police?"

"Telling the police would put them in danger," Hiram said. "They have no idea how to deal with mages."

"Except for the police that are mages!" Julian cried after a moment. "Bertram Elbe, he'll know how to handle this."

Hiram smiled at his enthusiasm and saw that a piece of his blond hair had fallen out of place, but the observation was not followed with his usual desire to smooth it back to where it belonged.

"You go to speak with him," Phaedrus advised.

"And what will you do?" Julian asked.

"I'm going to find out if he's left Pickering or not," the demon said. "Mr. Reinhart will accompany me. It's always better to have a human along."

"Is it?" Julian asked.

"Green skin can make people nervous," Phaedrus said. "Do either of you have the time?"

Julian reached into his coat and produced a pocket watch. "Quarter past one. Shall we reconvene at three, let's say? Your place," he said to Hiram. "It might be a little more private."

They all nodded in agreement, and Julian set off, leaving the other two standing just outside Blackwell's house.

ONCE JULIAN had gone his own way, Hiram looked at Phaedrus and asked, "How are we going to find out where he's gone?"

"Eddie said he had his sights on the oldest daughter of the De Launcier family," Phaedrus said.

"Right."

"I imagine we can find them."

Hiram said nothing.

"Or can we not?" Phaedrus asked after a moment.

"No...I can. The father is a mage. And one of the sisters, I believe. We'll have to ask around."

They stood together for a moment.

"Are we waiting for something?" they asked.

"I'm thinking," Hiram responded. "I've never seen Mr. De Launcier at the meeting house or the workshop."

"I thought he was a mage."

"Well, yes, but there are mages and then there are *mages*," Hiram said.

"And he's of the second sort?"

Hiram nodded.

"How do we find him?" Phaedrus asked.

"I think I know where to look," Hiram said and set off.

Phaedrus followed him, lagging behind for a few steps, then catching up to walk beside him. "I don't hold with these modern courting rituals."

Hiram glanced at them. "What?"

"The formality of it. It is a lot of coy nonsense, and I won't tolerate it," they said. "I thought you might want to know going forward."

"I thought we were waiting to see if we can retrieve my books and come out of this venture alive," Hiram said.

"Yes, but that's when I thought it would be over in time for supper," Phaedrus said.

"I see," Hiram replied, and neither of them said anything else on the subject, walking together quietly.

Hiram stopped before a building with smoked glass windows and a sign marked with a pale green and silver orb. It gave the place's name as the Will of the Wisp, though it had not been written in the Latin alphabet.

Phaedrus stared at the sign for a minute, their mouth silently moving to sound out the runes, and then said, "I always liked when people called them hinkypunks. Sounds sort of endearing."

"If I'm correct, the Owl Club meets here."

"Owl Club? Sort of grim. I don't know if we should get involved, given our recent stroke of luck."

"What do you mean? It's a gentleman's club, of a sort. Composed of mages, yes, but nothing dangerous."

"Owls are harbingers of death," Phaedrus said.

Hiram frowned. "I've always heard that owls are wise."

Phaedrus said, softly and to themself, "Oh, yes, Athena. How we love our Western literature here."

"Says the demon who tells Irish folktales," Hiram said to himself.

"The Celts have a special place in my heart. No place will make you believe in the mystic like those islands," Phaedrus said. "Anyway, are we going in?"

Hiram nodded and entered. The dim light made it

difficult to discern who had gathered there that day, but as they walked to the counter, Hiram tried to see if he recognized anyone. The man behind the counter asked, "What will it be?"

"I'm looking for someone," Hiram said.

"Aren't we all," the barkeep said, looking at Phaedrus.

Phaedrus looked back, training their eyes on the barkeep's blue ones, not blinking.

"Stop," Hiram said. "I'm looking for Mr. De Launcier. I believe his club meets here. Are they in?"

"I can bring a message with his next drink if you like," the man offered. "What should I say it's regarding?"

"A mutual friend," Hiram said.

The barkeep hummed. "He's having gin and tonic today."

Hiram glanced at Phaedrus, who set an appropriate amount of money on the counter. The barkeep took it, made the drink, and walked away.

Hiram offered, "I'll reimburse you. And for the doctor's as well."

"Don't bother," Phaedrus said, "I've got a book out that's doing rather well."

"A book! What's it called?"

"I'd rather not say," the creature said, "I like to keep my pen name separate from my personal life."

"Is it a famous book?"

Phaedrus didn't answer.

"It is, isn't it?"

"It's doing rather well," they said and offered no more information on the subject.

The barkeep returned and said, "Through that back door. Mr. De Launcier is waiting."

Together they thanked the man and headed through the back door, where a man in his fifties sat at a table, the drink they had sent in his hand.

"Sit, please. I hear you're looking for someone. Is Mr. Blackwell a mutual friend?" De Launcier asked.

They sat.

Hiram said, "We are more acquaintances than friends,

introduced through Mr. Candace. I lent Mr. Blackwell a book, and I had wished to use it as a reference, but I cannot locate him. I stopped by his house earlier today and found no one home."

"Mr. Blackwell has gone out of town for a while."

"Do you know where?" Hiram asked, but De Launcier was staring at Phaedrus, making them fidget uncomfortably.

He cleared his throat.

The older man asked, "What book did you lend him?"

"Three volumes concerning unholy creatures," Hiram said. "It's been in my family for generations."

"Three volumes written in an outdated script?" De Launcier asked.

"He's spoken of it to you?"

"He wanted to know if I knew where he could find a dictionary to aid in his reading, I told him I'd never seen the writing system before in my life. They're your books?"

"Yes."

"He didn't tell me his destination, but he must be going somewhere less provincial to find a dictionary," De Launcier said. "He should be home soon, I imagine. I hope it isn't a very pressing matter."

"No, no. Just a research question," Hiram said, "Thank you for your time."

He stood, knowing he was being rude, and left; Phaedrus was left behind for a moment but hurried to catch up with him. "What's the hurry, Hiram? We still don't know where he is."

"But I know what he's looking for," Hiram said.

"I hope it helps as much as you think it will," the creature said under their breath.

Hiram pressed his lips together and said nothing, knowing that what he said would be unkind unless he waited. Together they went to Hiram's home, and his heart sank when he saw that the place was still a mess, things scattered across the floor.

"Tell me it doesn't always look like this," Phaedrus said.

"No."

"I suppose we have time before Julian comes," they said and entered the house, stooping to pick things up off the floor.

Hiram joined them, having the distinct feeling that items were missing and feeling sweaty and stupid each time he tried to pick something up with his missing hand.

After less than five minutes the door opened.

They turned to see a black woman bearing a rifle in the doorway.

She studied them for a moment, then lowered the gun. "Figured you were dead at this point."

"No, Mrs. Burns, not dead," he said.

"People been coming, snooping around, looking through your things. Me and Mr. Burns did a pretty good job scaring them off, though."

"Thank you," he said.

"I'm afraid they did make off with some stuff, but I have my suspicions if you want to know who took it," said Mrs. Burns. "Woulda locked the door, except I haven't got a key."

"We don't have anything of great value," he said, "Except for my books, and they're all in order."

"Linens and the like, I think," said Mrs. Burns, "And food. It woulda gone bad anyway. Mr. Burns and me helped ourselves to some. Hope you don't mind."

"Better to come home to empty shelves than rotten food, I expect," he said.

"Where's your hand got to?"

He looked down. "An accident."

"Some accident," she said. "You all settled in here?"

"Yes, thank you for looking out for us," he said.

She nodded and left.

He and Phaedrus returned to picking up the house. He found that while some of their nicer plates and linens were missing, most things could be accounted for once he had things organized. He returned clothes to wardrobes and double-checked to make sure the rest of his books were still in place.

"Everything in order?" Phaedrus asked, surveying the house for things that had been missed.

"It seems so."

"You've got a lot of beds in here, Mr. Reinhart," the creature said, peeking their head into the two bedrooms.

"Three beds," Hiram said. "That is not a lot."

"One for you and your lonely nights," Phaedrus said, "And two for...?"

"Ellen and Hannah share the larger bed. Cassie has the other to herself."

"And they are?" Phaedrus asked.

"Ellen is my niece, Hannah is her mother and Cassie is her grandmother."

"A family?" the creature asked.

Hiram nodded.

"Goodness, I didn't imagine that you had a family," they said. "You have a niece and her mother...is the mother not your sister?"

"Ellen's father was my brother."

"Was?"

"Joshua is dead."

"Oh," the creature said and peered into the bedrooms again. "Now, Hiram, considering the dark complexion of the people in this neighborhood, a complexion which you do not share, and keeping in mind that your family owned the plantation that held June—"

"Yes," Hiram said.

"You didn't let me finish."

"They were slaves. Isn't that what you were going to ask? My father abused Cassie throughout his life, and Joshua was the result of that. He kept her close, in the house, near enough so that he could do what he wanted to her without having to walk too far," he said. "A common practice among other planters of our standing."

"Oh."

"Oh," Hiram repeated. He walked away and arranged the

chair around the table. "Feel free to have a seat, if you like."

Phaedrus sat. "You're from Georgia?"

"Yes."

"That's...very far south?"

"Deep," Hiram said. "Very deep."

"I haven't been to the United States since before they were united," Phaedrus said. "I prefer the Old World."

"Then why are you here?"

"I needed a change of scenery. I spent much too long touring the continent."

Hiram tilted his head. "But you said you prefer it?"

"Truth be told, I am a wanted individual."

"For what?" Hiram asked, finding himself more intrigued than he should have been.

"I made off with several items of value," they said with a degree of pride. "Gemstones, a decent amount of cash, family heirlooms, and several high-quality paintings."

"Phaedrus!" Hiram said, grinning and scandalized.

"I relocated, as a matter of course. This was years ago, but not so long that some grandchild won't remember what looney old grandpapa said. Maybe ten, fifteen more years before they've all forgotten my very distinct appearance."

"Consider me shocked. Why?"

They looked at their nails. "You don't really want to know."

"I do."

"You may recall that I've sworn off relationships."

"Intimate entanglements."

Phaedrus glanced up. "That was the exact phrase, wasn't it? Anyway, before that, I took things on my way out; I suppose I must have considered the things I took to be reparations for the...uh. Humiliation feels like an overly strong word, but it is humiliating to have someone...for them to ask..."

"You don't have to tell me," Hiram said, not really wanting them to continue; the creature had begun to struggle with their story, the words catching in their throat a little. "I stole twenty-nine people once."

Phaedrus smiled. "Must have been quite the caper."

Someone knocked at the door.

Hiram answered it, trying first with the wrong hand. "Hello, Julian. Come in."

Julian entered, and once seated, said, "I had a difficult time convincing Elbe that I was just dropping by to visit Blackwell, but he's investigating now. What did you two turn up?"

"He's looking for a dictionary," Hiram said, "For Germanic long-form. And I know who has one."

"You didn't say you knew who had one," Phaedrus pointed out.

"There are, to my knowledge, only four, and only one anywhere near us," Hiram said.

"In the possession of...?"

"Payton Reinhart, of the New York branch, a relative of mine," Hiram said.

"And what do we do with this knowledge?" Julian asked.

"I would, if possible, like to lay a trap for Blackwell."

"You mean go to New York and have your cousin put this book up for sale?" Julian asked.

"I don't expect you to accompany me. It could take a while," Hiram said, "and you have a family to which you must attend."

"You shouldn't go alone," Julian said.

"He doesn't have to," said Phaedrus; both men looked at them, but they offered no elaboration.

Hiram assumed they thought their intentions clear enough.

"And I will be with family," Hiram said.

Julian reached over and placed a hand on Hiram's arm. "Promise me that you'll be safe. You're a good man to have around."

"I'll be fine."

"When will you go?" Julian asked.

"I plan to leave in the morning."

"Make it the afternoon," Phaedrus said.

Julian nodded. "Write to me. I want to know you're safe."

Hiram smiled.

"I mean it." He glanced between the other two, then the door. He hesitated before he announced, "I'll leave you to your preparations, then. Let me know if you need anything."

"Thank you," Hiram said and saw him to the door.

"Good luck, Hiram." Julian patted his shoulder.

"Thank you."

Julian left, and Hiram looked at Phaedrus.

"What?" the creature asked.

"Are you leaving too?"

"No," they said and shook their head. They ran their hands through their hair, combing it over their shoulder then tucking it behind their ear. "Do you plan on sleeping here tonight?"

"Is there a reason I shouldn't?"

"You haven't got any food, and I think someone stole your quilt."

"Ah. I'll take one of the other ones."

"Dinner, then, on me," Phaedrus said. "Come along." They stood and headed out before Hiram could protest.

Hiram locked the door, using a spell as well as a key.

"If you don't mind me prying, how do you intend to finance this trip?" they asked.

"No idea."

"I thought as much. Good thing I'm coming," they said. "A stagecoach to Toronto, and we'll find passage from there, steamship or the railway, I expect."

"I'll owe you a considerable sum."

"I am considering this an investment in my personal safety, no reimbursement needed," they said.

"That's...overly generous."

"You can owe me a favor if you'd prefer." Phaedrus gave Hiram a sideways glance. They smiled after a moment. "Have I made you blush?"

"No," he lied.

They raised their eyebrows, and he knew it hadn't been a convincing lie. Phaedrus walked a little bit in front of Hiram, leading him to a public-house, where they took a seat and Phaedrus ordered for both of them, two of the same meal.

"You'll like it," they promised. "Meat and potatoes, nothing to argue with."

While they waited for their food to arrive, Hiram asked, "What paintings did you steal?"

"Oh, I don't know. I sold them all years ago. I had expenses," they said.

"What sort of expenses?" Hiram asked.

Phaedrus looked him over, their eyes cold as careful consideration played out on their face.

Hiram began to worry he'd asked something very rude.

Finally, they shared, "I thought changing my form would soothe my anxieties about my place in the world. It worked for other people. I spent time and coin trying to shape my body to be the one that suited me best. More attempts than I care to recount."

Hiram struggled to keep his face neutral, the right combination of acceptance and disinterest. Phaedrus seemed to want that and prickled at anything else.

"I spent the last bit of that money starting over. A clean slate, I suppose. I realized that the body was not the source of my unease, not for me anyway. It followed no matter what I changed."

Hiram bobbed his head as he scrambled to think of something to say. Something that would not be intrusive or unkind or embarrassing. "I did read about that once. Changing bodies."

"Oh?"

"They guard their secrets so close at that university it's hard to know what's rumor and what's something they can really do."

"Not a rumor, but the mages who work such spells are hard to come by. It's highly specialized and not so widely needed as other practices."

"Hmm." Hiram drifted off into thoughts about what type of magic would be required to transform a person in such a way. He knew almost nothing about medical magic but had some experience with transforming objects. He shuddered to think about what could go wrong.

Phaedrus said, "I did keep some of the jewelry, though."

"Such as?"

They removed a ring from their finger and handed Hiram a ring set with a large diamond flanked with sapphires. "Pretty, isn't it?"

"Very."

"It's worth a tidy sum."

Hiram had a fair idea of how much a ring like that would cost. His mother had worn jewelry, and she'd donned attractively gaudy gems when his father had hosted parties. Hiram's father had showered his mother in pretty things, either to keep her happy or show her off or both. Hiram didn't know. He'd been too young. He only remembered his mother in a lovely dress with glittering jewels, her hair done to perfection and her eyes just as bright as the stones she wore.

A woman dropped off their food, and Phaedrus gestured for Hiram to start eating. He tried, struggling until Phaedrus pulled his plate away, cut his food for him and slid it back.

"I didn't consider that you might have difficulties," they said.

"I forget too," Hiram said.

"Should have gotten the stew," Phaedrus said, taking their own fork back up and continuing to eat. "I'll keep that in mind."

Hiram didn't know what to say; he didn't want to sound petulant and tell them he could manage his own affairs, nor did he want to seem childish and in need of tending. He didn't say much as he ate.

Phaedrus was similarly quiet, though they seemed to be in contemplation about something.

"What are you thinking about?" Hiram asked.

"Pondering what the future holds for me," they said. "I

hope this venture proves successful."

Hiram nodded.

"You haven't been talkative either."

"I lied. I do miss my hand," he said.

Phaedrus smiled. "You seem adaptable. Surely this life you lead is much different from the one you had in the rolling hills of Georgia."

"How did you know I was from the Red Hills?"

"Does all of Georgia not have hills?"

"The Red Hills is a specific area, though, and that's where I grew up," he said. "That's what people mean, usually, when they talk about Georgia's hills."

"I assumed the whole state was hilly," they admitted.

Hiram smiled and then said, "It's much colder here. Snow? God, I hate the snow. I could write books about it."

"We aren't even that far north."

Hiram shook his head. "I can't imagine anything being snowier or colder than this."

Phaedrus looked at their emptied plates, left an appropriate amount of money on the table and stood. "I'll walk you home."

The mage stood as well, and they walked side by side the whole way, Phaedrus with their hands in the pockets of their trousers. They followed Hiram inside, glanced around the small house once more and made a sound that seemed disapproving.

"Is something wrong?" Hiram asked.

"You plan on sleeping here?"

"Yes."

Phaedrus looked around and stated, "I need to return to my boarding house and arrange for my things to be put in storage."

"Oh."

"It was what I planned to do in the morning."

"And?"

"And it would be much easier to do if I woke up there in the morning," Phaedrus said. "And your home is very dreary."

Hiram frowned, feeling there was a part of the conversation Phaedrus had neglected to share. "So I suppose you should return there."

Phaedrus fixed their eyes on his face and said in a tone that made Hiram think he had said something stupid, "So then you do plan to sleep here."

"Yes? Unless you think I should plan otherwise."

"I do think that."

Hiram blinked several times. "Where do you think I should sleep?"

"I'm glad you asked," Phaedrus said. "Do you own a suitcase?"

"As long as it hasn't been stolen," he said.

"Pack for our trip," they said.

Hiram went, trying to figure out what was happening. He thought of a few answers, but they all seemed unlikely, considering what the creature had said. Hiram considered, as he struggled to buckle the suitcase shut, that Phaedrus had given him what could be considered conflicting messages.

He checked on his books, locked the trunk, and whispered a few protection spells over it.

He reemerged from his bedroom with the suitcase, set it down and walked outside, knocking on the door of Mr. and Mrs. Burns.

Mr. Burns answered and asked, "What can I do ya for?"

"I'm going on a trip. The house will be locked, but I would appreciate it if you and Mrs. Burns could continue to keep an eye out for me."

"Course we can, no problem."

"I can't express my gratitude enough," he said.

"Haven't seen the women around much," Mr. Burns said.

"I sent them ahead. I'll be joining them shortly."

"Yeah?"

"We'll be visiting friends in the country."

Mr. Burns nodded. "Sounds nice. Need anything else?"

"No, that's it, thank you," Hiram said. He stepped back and Mr. Burns closed the door. Hiram returned to his home and found that Phaedrus had taken up his suitcase.

"Ready?" they asked.

Hiram nodded.

Phaedrus carried his suitcase the whole way, though Hiram offered to take it several times and the third time got as a response a fable about a monkey and a dolphin in which the dolphin drowns the monkey for lying.

Hiram did not ask again after that.

He shifted nervously outside the door of Phaedrus' rented room as they unlocked the door; they stepped inside and motioned for Hiram to follow. They placed Hiram's suitcase by the door and said, "I need to pack as well. Make yourself comfortable."

The demon gestured around the room, and Hiram took that to mean that he could sit wherever he wanted. He took a seat in an armchair and tried not to stare at the things that littered the room: more jewelry, bottles of perfume, small figurines, and statuettes made of ivory and jade, as well as fine clothes made of silks and satins and leather-bound books with gilded edges.

Hiram had not noticed these things the first time in this room, too preoccupied with the creature and the danger at hand. If he had noticed them, they surely would have set him aching for home.

"There are facilities at the end of the hall, should you need them," the demon said without looking at Hiram, absorbed in their packing, carefully selecting what they would need. "Do you think we'll be going anywhere nice?"

"It's a possibility. My cousins have retained their family fortune."

They nodded and adjusted their approach.

"Why have you brought me here?" Hiram asked.

The creature turned to look at him, a half-folded nightshirt in their hands. They set the shirt aside, crossed their arms, and asked, "Why do you think?"

"I don't know."

"But what do you *think?*" they asked again.

"You were adamant that if I were to see you undressed, I would think differently of you," Hiram said. "And you didn't seem enthusiastic."

"And you won't see me undressed," they assured him. "I'm not convinced at all that you don't now think of me as a, um, a...well, I'd rather not say it..." They sighed and hesitated, then finally said, "As a certain type of person in unusual clothing. Especially given your previous statement of preference for those of a particular sex."

"I've never met anyone that wasn't, uh..."

"One thing or the other?" Phaedrus asked.

Hiram nodded.

"And so you're curious," they said tiredly and took up their nightshirt again.

"No, that's not it," Hiram said, "It's...I didn't know."

Phaedrus turned away.

Hiram sighed, wondered if he should stand, but remained seated. "I think you're tired, Phaedrus. I think you haven't been sleeping. You *look* like you haven't been sleeping."

They glanced back briefly and said, "My nights have been restless."

"I'm frightened. I think you are too. I think that's why you brought me here. I know that I feel safer when there's someone else nearby. If I were at home alone right now, I'd be jumpier than a cat on hot bricks."

Phaedrus licked their lips, turned back to him, and tucked a piece of hair behind their ear. "You've got me. I am frightened."

"Understandable."

"Working on my second draft one minute, in the basement of a lunatic murderer the next," they said. "Now it's liable to happen again at any moment."

The mage considered telling them that Blackwell would need the dictionary, probably, before he could summon them again, but he didn't think it would soothe their worries. Instead, he stood, walked over to the desk and opened the jewelry box. He peered into it for a moment and then selected a short, silver chain with a small, circular pendant. Upon examination, he saw that the pendant was a coin.

"Do you mind?" Hiram asked.

"Mind what? Do you know what that is?"

"A coin?"

"An Irish groat minted under Henry VIII," Phaedrus told.

"Oh. I won't hurt it."

The creature rubbed their eyes and asked, "But what do you intend to *do* with it?"

"Enchant it so that I would be able to find you if he did manage to summon you again."

Phaedrus came over, took the necklace from him, and returned it. "I couldn't abide having to wear that all the time."

"Silver's best."

Phaedrus hummed an acknowledgment and handed him another silver necklace, longer and more delicate, with a small, crooked star. "This should do."

He cupped it in his hand and whispered to it for several minutes, then returned it to the creature, saying, "I'd put it on for you..."

Phaedrus clasped it around their neck. "I understand. Did you use that spell often? You seem to have it memorized."

"Um," Hiram said, wondering if the truth would be offensive. "We had several cats on the plantation and a few dogs. After Walter went missing and didn't come back for weeks, I fitted them all with collars with that enchantment."

The creature laughed.

"He came back in terrible shape, and I thought that if I'd been able to find him sooner..."

"Of course, perfectly understandable. Do you see that stack of trunks?" they asked.

Hiram followed their gaze and nodded.

"Start putting things in them, if you would be so kind."

Hiram nodded and pulled the top trunk down; it landed with a thud, and the creature jumped, turning to look at him with a hand on their chest.

"Sorry," the mage said.

"I would have gotten it for you," they said. "Anyway, I'll finish packing this, and then I'll help you. Start with everything in that wardrobe." They turned away, back to their suitcase, then turned back and said, "Don't worry about trying to fold things."

Hiram nodded but tried to fold things anyway, wondering if there was a spell for this. By the time Phaedrus finished, he had sloppily folded half the contents of the wardrobe. They peered into the trunk disapprovingly but said nothing.

"I'll do the desk," they said and took down the second trunk.

By the time they had filled the four trunks, with a short break for supper, the room seemed much more squalid than it had before; they weren't, as Hiram had noticed before, in a very nice part of town. Money didn't seem to be an issue for Phaedrus, so Hiram guessed either they had a hard time going undisturbed in nicer areas or they preferred something about a place like this.

"Storage in the morning," they said, looking at the trunks then kneeling beside Hiram to do the buckles on the last one.

"I almost had it," he said.

"It's about time anyway that I moved on."

"From the boarding house?" Hiram asked.

Phaedrus shrugged. "This town has started to leave a bad taste in my mouth."

"Oh," the mage said, feeling unreasonably disappointed.

"It has been a long time since I've lived in the country," they mused. They gathered a few things, including a toothbrush, and left the room without a word. When they returned, they reminded him, "Facilities are at the end of the hall. Knock when you return."

Hiram struggled to unbuckle the straps of his suitcase, and Phaedrus watched, not offering to help. He finally retrieved the items he needed and went to the end of the hall, washing his face and cleaning his teeth. He spent some time examining himself in the mirror. Burns showed plainly on his neck, and his eye remained bloodshot from when Blackwell had pierced it. That would heal, he was sure, though he didn't know the extent to which he would be scarred.

He returned, almost opening the door, then stopped and knocked.

"One moment," the creature said and opened the door for him a little while later. They had changed into an unadorned nightshirt and had a hairbrush in hand. Even dressed plainly, there was still something that defied categorization about them. He did not dare to look too long, lest he be accused of staring again.

Hiram returned his things to his suitcase while Phaedrus brushed and then began to braid their hair. He took out a nightshirt as well and glanced at Phaedrus.

"Would you like me to avert my eyes?" they asked.

Hiram couldn't tell if he was being mocked.

He thought about answering 'no' but said, "It doesn't matter to me," and began to change. In the past few days, he had better learned how to dress and undress, needing to jump and wiggle more than he had beforehand.

Phaedrus watched him for a few minutes then asked, "Do you need help?'

"Not unless it is your intention to always help me undress," Hiram said. "I don't mean to sound ungrateful, but I will live the rest of my life without this hand and more than likely without anyone helping me unbutton my trousers. I must learn to do it alone."

"That's a grim outlook for a young man."

"When one's feelings are unrequited in every venture, one develops a grim outlook," he said, pulling his nightshirt over his head and hissing when he attempted to push his stump through the sleeve too quickly.

"Self-pity is not attractive, Hiram," they admonished.

"It's not pity. It's practicality."

Phaedrus chuckled and turned back the bedcovers. "When you are done being practical, come to bed. I'm ready to retire."

Hiram hesitated.

"Compared to that closet, there is plenty of room," they said, "There are some who fit a family of four in such a bed."

He approached but remained uncertain. He had no personal qualms and even felt a flurry of eagerness but didn't want to misstep.

"Don't tell me you've grown shy."

"No, it's...you have boundaries, and I am not aware of where they lie."

Phaedrus settled under the covers and said, "I will let you know if you become inappropriate."

Hiram nodded and climbed into bed. The whole bed smelled of their perfume.

Phaedrus blew out the last candle, and together they lay in silence until the creature asked, "Do you believe this plan will work?"

"I hope it will. Even if it doesn't, Payton may have more insights into how to find Blackwell."

"Using what methods, I wonder."

"I don't care."

"Liar."

"I care very little," Hiram amended. "I will get my books back, and I will ensure that their power is not abused again."

"That sort of power is only meant to be abused," Phaedrus said.

"I'm aware," Hiram said. "Otherwise I would not be selling enchanted trinkets but living as prince of the mages with all sorts of unholy things bound to my will."

The creature laughed. "So noble you are!"

"It's what my father and grandfather did. It is not what I chose to do. I like to think choosing counts for something."

"Choosing to be a decent, normal person does not earn you anything."

Hiram sulked for a moment but considered that they might be right.

"But it isn't easy, either," they added, reaching out and

placing a hand on him for a moment. "Goodnight, Hiram." The dim light from their eyes vanished.

"Goodnight," he said and closed his eyes.

WHEN HIRAM woke in the morning, Phaedrus and all their things were gone except for the suitcase. He washed and dressed, and as he worked on tucking his shirt in, the creature returned, looking merrier than they had the day before.

"Did you sleep well?" he asked.

"Better than I have."

"Are your affairs arranged?"

The creature nodded and asked, "Are you ready to go? A stagecoach departs for Toronto in about an hour. I'd like to catch it."

Hiram nodded and finished dressing as quickly as he could, then took up his suitcase and followed Phaedrus, who chatted as they walked. "We could take a coach the entire way, but there are other options—steamships and the railway."

Hiram did not know what to say and uselessly added, "I traveled by ship to get here."

"The railway would be quicker," Phaedrus said, "We are in a sort of a rush."

"And the stagecoach is safer, I believe. Have you heard about the sort of things that happen on railways? Will I have time to write a letter? I should write to my cousin."

Phaedrus paused and thought for a moment. "We'll stop at the post office, then head..." they paused, staring at the ground.

"What?"

"Look down and tell me if you see the same thing I do."

Hiram looked at the ground and saw a familiar face reflected in a small puddle. He crouched. "June?"

"Hello, Hiram...and Phaedrus. Didn't expect you. What are your plans for the next few days?"

"Traveling to New York," Hiram answered.

"Hmm, well...your gravestone changed."

"What?"

"It used to be you lived to be fifty-one."

"That's it?" Hiram balked.

"Shh. The date has changed. I shouldn't be telling you this, but...so help me if I let you die at twenty-six."

"Do you visit my grave often?"

"I know the man who tends the graveyard. Just...be very careful, please. I hope this helps."

"Thank you."

"Got to go, *be safe*, Hiram," June urged. His face disappeared.

Phaedrus said, "He'll get in a lot of trouble for that. Don't expect any more messages."

Hiram stood up.

"I planned very much on taking the railway," Phaedrus admitted, looking Hiram over, "whether you agreed or not, as I am the one financing this. But now it appears that might have been a rash choice."

Hiram followed them when they walked away, not knowing what to say. He penned a short letter at the post office.

"Is that your best writing?" Phaedrus asked disapprovingly. "Oh...you didn't lose your writing hand, did you? I'm sorry!"

"No, this is my writing hand," he said.

He felt Phaedrus watching him as he sealed the envelope

and addressed it. He borrowed money for postage and sent the letter. As they walked out, the creature asked, "Nerves, isn't it? You're shaking."

"I did recently have someone from the future warn me of my impending death."

"And then I decided not to take a train."

"It is unsettling nevertheless."

The demon reached out and put a hand on his shoulder. "Hiram, I'm *extremely* sure that you will survive this."

"Why?"

"Because I'm going to keep you alive," they said, then smiled and patted his cheek. "Let's go. We might still have time to eat something if we hurry."

They did have time to eat and arrived at the station in time to buy tickets for a ride that they would share with six other people. They loaded their luggage and Phaedrus pushed their way to the front of the line and whispered to Hiram, "Let me sit against the wall if you will. I don't want anyone next to me."

"Someone will have to be next to you," Hiram said.

"Yes, you," they said. "I meant anyone else."

"Oh."

"And I'm going to be very rude and pretend to sleep the whole time so that no one can talk to me," they warned.

"Not even me?" Hiram asked with a smile, settling next to the creature on the bench; they had acquired the seat next to the wall.

"I am not in the mood," they said.

Hiram nodded.

The other six passengers filed in, all polite and proper, leaving Hiram to feel like a savage for pushing through with Phaedrus. He glanced at the creature, who had already closed their eyes and leaned against the wall.

The coach stopped every few hours to change horses, giving the passengers the chance to find food, stretch their legs or do other necessary things. Hiram took each opportunity to move around, and when he grew hungry, he stared after the food of others until the demon took notice and offered to buy him something.

When they offered, Hiram declined politely, saying "No, thank you."

Phaedrus squinted. "Are you sure?"

"Yes."

They titled their head, then walked away and returned with something wrapped in greasy newspaper. "The woman claimed it was mutton," they said when they saw Hiram eying the meat pie.

"Oh."

They took a bite, then nodded. "Definitely mutton." They took one more bite, then handed it to Hiram. "Here, you finish it, I'm not as hungry as I thought."

"No, I—" he tried to protest, but they took his hand and placed the newspaper bundle into it.

"There's no need to be proud," they said softly, "I've known what it is to want for something in your belly."

Hiram looked at the food in his hand.

"Not currently, of course. You can see I've gone a little soft around the middle."

Hiram glanced at their stomach, hidden by loosely fitted clothes, and wondered what they would look like without them. He blushed and turned his attention to his lunch, looking away and walking back toward the carriage. He tried to push aside the licentious thoughts the comment had provoked, trying not to think of whether their body would be pliant or firm, if they had any more freckles.

"Unlike you," they said. "Very narrow, especially about the hips. But you seem to be the sort of person who will always run to thinness."

Hiram looked over and brushed a bit of crumb off his mouth with his wrist; he swallowed and said, "Yes, it's a strong family trait. My brother was built as I was. I often wonder if Ellen will be or if she'll take after her mother more."

Phaedrus said nothing but did reach out and brush something from Hiram's shirt. "Are you always a sloppy eater?"

"One hand," he said and finished eating, then crumpled the paper and threw it away. He brushed more crumbs off himself. He glanced at the coach they were supposed to depart from and said, "We ought to head back."

"I might scream," they said. "The jostling! Let's go." They tugged on Hiram's sleeve, and Hiram happily followed along.

The trip had been dull so far, full of people sharing typical small talk and giving Phaedrus inquisitive glances.

When they returned to the coach, there were no seats left by the wall, and Phaedrus hesitated, touching Hiram on the leg. Hiram glanced back, then looked at the young woman with a baby in her arms who sat against the wall; there were two seats left in the middle of two different benches.

"Excuse me, ma'am?" he asked.

"No, don't," Phaedrus hissed.

The woman looked at Hiram.

"I'm very sorry to ask you, my traveling companion runs the risk of being ill if not seated against the wall and, given the arrangement of the coach, I was hoping you could allow them to have your seat."

"Oh...I..."

"Don't mind him, please. He's a terrible worrier," Phaedrus said. "I'll be perfectly fine."

The woman stared at him, and the baby gurgled. "No, I...I can move over. It's a very small matter to move over."

"Thank you," Hiram said.

She began to get up, then looked at the other middle seat and asked, "Did you two wish to sit together?"

"If it's not too much trouble."

She shook her head and moved seats, leaving two spaces for them and taking the middle seat on the middle bench.

Phaedrus took their seat against the wall and Hiram took his in the middle. Neither of them spoke any further with the young woman, but her baby did gurgle and wave at them; given the age of the child, Hiram couldn't be sure there was any intention in the waving. The child began to scream inconsolably after about an hour.

The other passengers began to give her dirty looks and mutter unkind things to each other.

The demon sat up, sighing, unable to continue their sham of a nap. They rubbed their eyes and frowned at the baby. They glanced at the mother and color went to her cheeks.

"Hand the little one over," Phaedrus said.

"She's only colicky," the mother said.

"Would you like her not to be?" they asked.

"Forgive my companion," Hiram said.

"No, don't forgive me, hand me the child," they said, leaning over. "I'm very good with babies."

The woman, looking terrified, handed over the still screaming child.

"Name?"

"Charlotte."

"Hmm, all right." The creature examined the infant, then whispered to her and gave her a few pats on the back.

The baby quieted and let out a small coo. She knotted her hand in Phaedrus's hair.

They untangled their locks from the baby's hand. To the mother, they said, "A temporary reprieve, but it should last the night." Phaedrus touched the child's cheek and handed her back.

"How did you...?"

"Old family secret," Phaedrus said, crossed their arms and nestled back against the seat.

The child remained quiet for the rest of the ride.

Two stops later, they arrived in Toronto.

Hiram hopped up and down as Phaedrus led him to the nearest tavern.

"What are you doing?"

"My leg's gone numb," Hiram said.

"Well, stop," they said, giving him a look of disapproval. "And tell me, Mr. Reinhart, do you wish me to book separate rooms?"

"Only if that is what you would prefer," Hiram said.

Phaedrus didn't inform him of their choice until they requested only one room at the tavern. They were brought to a room and set down their suitcases; Hiram glanced at Phaedrus and Phaedrus looked back.

"What?" they asked.

Hiram shook his head.

"Hiram, talking is important," they said.

"I'm worried about what June said."

As they played with their necklace, they said, "I told you I wasn't going to let you die."

"What if we both die?"

"Together?" Phaedrus asked, one eyebrow raised. "How tragic."

Hiram rubbed his eyes. "I don't *want* to be tragic."

The creature sat on the bed, pulling up their legs and crossing them. "What do you want?"

"I'm not sure."

"You're young. You are allowed to be uncertain," they reassured him. "We should have something to eat before bed."

"Would you mind..."

"Would I mind what?" they prompted.

"If I came to sit beside you?"

"No," they said and patted the bed.

Hiram went to sit next to them and sighed. He sat awkwardly for a moment, lacking the courage needed to do what he wanted. He'd never done it before and didn't know how to proceed.

"I'm going to die," he said, looking at his hand, not completing the thought. *I'm going to die unloved.* He wondered if that would have always been his fate, to die unloved at fifty-one or twenty-six.

"Shush," Phaedrus scolded and put an arm around him. "Have I told you like your accent?"

"I haven't got an accent."

"Oh, you do," they said, "And I like it."

Hiram said nothing.

"Now tell me something you like about me."

"Your laugh."

"Your curls," Phaedrus said and pulled Hiram close, pressing their lips to his curls. "I have always had a weakness for curls."

When they pulled back, Hiram met their eyes and leaned in a little.

"Don't, Hiram, please."

Hiram nodded.

"It's not that I don't like you."

"But you don't believe that my affection for you is genuine," Hiram hazarded.

Phaedrus moved back, then stood. They took a few steps, glanced at Hiram, and asked, "What do you think I am, Hiram? I know you can parrot what I've told you I am, but tell me honestly, if your affection is real, what you expect me to be."

"I think..." Hiram hesitated and took a moment to seriously consider his answer. He stood when he had finished thinking and took a step towards Phaedrus. "I believe that you are what June is. An angel. Fallen now, of course. And that is something otherworldly, something that I cannot understand."

"You're avoiding the question," they pointed out sourly.

"A person."

"Hiram, you're being difficult." They turned away from him and sat on the bed, their arms crossed.

"Because you're asking me to guess at what body parts you have, and I don't want to do that. Any answer I give would upset you because that's not what you want me to think about," he said, hoping that Phaedrus would abandon the topic.

"The truth," Phaedrus insisted.

"The truth is that you have a body that appears human," Hiram began, then continued, straightening his waistcoat. "Assuming that this resemblance is more than surface deep and given that there are two common sets of body parts designated to the sexes *and* considering that nature will even mix these sets with frequency enough that it is fairly common knowledge, there are a variety of configurations that your body could have. You've even mentioned previously that you've paid for magics meant to change you and to reverse those changes. Taking that into consideration, any guess I might make would be less than educated."

Phaedrus blinked.

"The larger truth is that when I look at you, I am not wondering about which body parts you might have. I am wondering..." Hiram lost his nerve a little here, his face growing hot. "I am wondering about...I don't know! About you. About...sensations."

The demon laughed and held out their hand, pulling Hiram close once he had taken it; they folded Hiram into their arms. "You are so innocent, aren't you? Such a kind little soul He stuffed into this skinny body."

"And I like your perfume," Hiram said.

Phaedrus squeezed him tighter. "I'm sorry if I act as though I'm trying to push you away."

"You're following me to New York and paying for it. If you're trying to push me away, you're doing a horrible job."

"I am worried, for my own life, for yours. I worry that we might have very little time together, and I worry that if I act on that fear, I will move things too quickly. Especially given that you come from a time when young men of standing cannot do more than stroll with a young lady without proposing."

Hiram giggled.

"What?"

"Trying to court you would be a nightmare, I imagine."

"On the contrary, I'm very easy to persuade in carnal matters," Phaedrus said, sounding disappointed with themself. "Or...I was."

"Just as well that you aren't. I don't have anything for you to steal."

The creature laughed and kissed Hiram's hair again. "We really must eat and get to bed. We will spend the day traveling again."

They released Hiram and stood, taking him by the hand and leading him downstairs, where they ordered stew for him. Both of them ate, used the facilities, and changed into nightclothes as they had the previous night, with Phaedrus maintaining their privacy and then watching Hiram fight with his clothing.

Once he had changed, they patted the bed.

Hiram went over, climbing under the covers.

Phaedrus pulled the covers up to his shoulders.

They both lay on their side, facing each other.

"Close your eyes, go to sleep," the creature said.

Hiram obeyed but opened his eyes when he heard a lot of rustling and found that the creature had come closer to him.

"I said close your eyes," Phaedrus said.

"Why?"

"Because you have to close your eyes to sleep," they said.

Hiram closed his eyes again and nestled into the pillow. He felt Phaedrus put a hand on his waist and he heard them move again, but this time kept his eyes closed. His nose filled up with the smell of their perfume and something pressed against his mouth; he felt reasonably sure that Phaedrus had kissed him. The fluttering in his stomach would be unwarranted otherwise.

"And you have to close your eyes when you kiss. It's unsettling otherwise," they said, nestling against his chest.

Hiram put an arm around them and prayed that neither of them would die.

THEY SPENT three more days traveling by coach. On the third night, Phaedrus tossed their suitcase aside and tumbled into bed. Hiram sat beside them, and before he could ask what troubled them, the demon, without sitting up, reached out and pulled him into their grip, wrapping him up in a hug that was much stronger than he had expected.

"Hiram, starting tomorrow we will take the train, and if we die, so be it. I cannot stand these coaches any longer."

"You're being dramatic."

"I am allowed to be dramatic," they said and squeezed him tighter.

Hiram grunted.

"What?"

"You're very strong."

"I haven't hurt you, have I?"

"No."

The creature pressed their lips to his forehead. "You may not like me much by the time this trip is over."

"I don't know why you would say that," Hiram said. "It isn't as though you've been rude and irritable recently."

They released him and rolled onto their back. "One day,

maybe two, of that jostling, but...what, five...six more days? I will become impossible to be around."

Hiram pushed himself up onto one elbow and looked at them for a little while, considering what he wanted to do, wondering if it would upset them. No more kisses had passed between the two of them, not on the mouth anyway, though a few times Hiram had thought he might be able to get away with it.

Now felt like one of those times. He leaned over and kissed Phaedrus on the cheek. The creature turned their face toward him, eyebrows raised, but said nothing. He pressed his mouth to theirs and they did not pull away, but turned toward him a little more, putting one hand on the back of his head.

Hiram attempted to touch their face but found himself falling short, forgetting that he did not have fingertips on that arm anymore. He pulled back and sighed.

Phaedrus brushed the pad of their thumb across his cheek and then his lips. "Does it trouble you? When we arrive in New York, you should have a doctor examine it again."

He nodded and thought that an infection could be the cause of the death about which June had warned him.

"You're worrying again," they said.

"Perhaps."

"Do you plan to stay with your family?" they asked.

"It's likely that they'll invite me to stay with them."

"Will they invite me as well?"

"Payton will insist."

"Do you think?"

"I am certain."

"And will we be allowed to continue sharing a room, or will your family frown on it?" they asked.

Hiram thought and answered carefully, "Knowing what I do of this branch and of my cousin, it will not matter to any of them if you and I share a bed."

"Not even a little?"

"Not unless one of them sets their sights on you. Payton is married, though that may not prove a deterrent."

Phaedrus nodded.

Hiram kissed them again, thinking that he could spend hours doing this, wanting to cover every inch of the creature with his mouth. He put his mouth to their neck and Phaedrus pulled back sharply.

"I'm sorry," Hiram said, "I—"

"No, stop fretting. You nosed one of my burns."

"Oh! I'm so sorry!" he said.

Phaedrus shushed him and left one more kiss on his mouth. "Are you hungry?"

"A little."

"Something for supper and then to bed. Another early morning followed by many arduous hours of travel await us."

Hiram nodded, then, instead of getting up, kissed the creature, more insistently than he had before, wrapping an arm around them and pulling them close. Phaedrus didn't resist and after a moment, they pushed closer to him, climbing half on top of him and opening their mouth against his.

That deep kiss did not last as long as Hiram would have liked.

Phaedrus moved back and shook their head. "No more, not right now."

Hiram nodded, sitting up a little bit.

"It wouldn't be any good for either of us to become overexcited."

"No, of course not," Hiram agreed raggedly.

They stood, straightened their clothes and headed for the door.

Hiram followed and took their hand. The abrupt end to that excitement, the distance between them, felt sharp and hollow all at once.

Phaedrus looked back, regarding him warily. "What?"

"I didn't want to leave yet."

"I said no more," Phaedrus reprimanded and pulled their hand back from his.

"I'd like a moment," he confessed, "to catch my breath before we go to eat."

"Then take a moment," they said, their voice softening, but just barely.

Hiram looked at the floor and, feeling unusually warm, said, "I did intend to embrace you as well."

"You may," the creature said.

Hiram put his arms around them and closed his eyes, intentionally taking slow breaths and wondering if his gravestone had changed again. "I'm sorry."

Phaedrus' fingers stroked the back of his neck. "You really meant it when you said you hadn't been with anyone."

"Yes."

"Not even a kiss."

"Not like that." Hiram had never felt such an exquisite embarrassment at his inexperience.

Gently, they asked, "Are you ready now?"

"Yes."

They pulled back, running their hand along his arm and grasping his hand lightly before heading out the door.

In the morning, Phaedrus shook him awake but he didn't open his eyes. "Come now, Hiram, we have to continue this hellish trip."

Hiram pushed himself up and rubbed his eyes. "Would it be so terrible to miss one coach? Another one will come."

Phaedrus frowned and studied him for a while. They leaned in and pressed their lips to his forehead, then pulled back looking more concerned than they had before. "You're warm, Hiram."

Hiram rubbed his eyes, not knowing what to say.

"Oh."

"Oh?" he asked, not liking the way their pale eyes had gone wide.

"Oh your hand," they said, "Let me see it. Not the hand, the missing one."

Hiram held out his stump.

They began to unwind the bandages. "Have you been taking care of this?"

"As best I can."

Phaedrus set the bandages aside and shook their head, eyeing the way the skin around his stitches had become red and puffy.

Hiram stared too. "This is what kills me."

"Shut up, Hiram," they snapped and stood. "Stay here."

"Where are you going?"

"To fix this. Start a fire," they said and left without dressing.

Hiram remained in bed and tried to imagine the stir they would cause going about in a nightshirt. He attempted to examine the wound but had to turn his eyes away. He could not look at it for long, which, he supposed, might have been part of what had gotten him into this situation.

He piled wood into the grate and tried to figure out how he would use matches with only one hand before he recalled that he was a mage. He began the fire with a small spell, one that Cassie and Hannah surely would have frowned upon, and wondered again if they would be happier without him in their lives.

It wasn't that they fought or had any large disagreements about things, but he wondered if his presence, white and male, isolated them from others. People certainly thought that he was lying about Ellen being his niece, he knew that much. Was he, just by being there, keeping away those who would befriend them, or men who would court Hannah?

He would ask Susan. She would be honest with him, unafraid of hurting his feelings.

Phaedrus returned with their arms full and a foul look on their face.

"My mother died of an infection," he said.

"You're not going to die."

"You can't know that," he said and watched as Phaedrus poured spirits into a kettle and set it over the fire.

"You should have been taking better care of yourself."

"My apologies, I've never had to cut off my own hand before," he said mildly.

The creature looked at him but said nothing.

"Being the fine and clever mage you are, I don't imagine you know any spells for this sort of thing?" they asked after a while.

"Medicinal magic has been closely guarded for many years," Hiram said, "The university in Triviai has the only program for training in such things, and they are extremely picky."

"Stuck up, all of them," they scoffed. "No herbwives on your plantation?"

"If there were, they certainly kept it a secret."

They checked the kettle and frowned, then turned that frown toward Hiram. "Go wash, at any rate. Maybe we won't lose the whole day's travel."

Hiram went, and when he returned, Phaedrus asked, "How have you been tying your shoes?"

"I've been tucking the laces into the side."

The creature chuckled, then motioned for him to come over. "Might hurt," they warned.

Hiram nodded.

Phaedrus took his injured arm and held it gently. They dipped a cloth into the alcohol they had boiled and used it to wipe Hiram's stump, causing him to flinch and hiss every so often. They cleaned the area thoroughly and noted, "You'll need to have these stitches out soon. The next time we stop at something more than a roadside tavern, we will find you a doctor."

"In New York—"

"Too far. I'm not risking it. We should have waited longer to start this trip, waited until we knew your health would hold."

Hiram swallowed.

They dried off his wound and then began to spread something thick and golden onto it. Hiram stared, knowing that he should have recognized the substance, and the creature said, "Honey."

Hiram nodded as if that made sense to him.

They wrapped his arm again in clean bandages that, on

inspection, proved to be torn sheets. They looked at his stump and said, "There. That should do, I expect."

Hiram nodded. "Thank you."

"You live long enough, and you pick a few things up. I haven't got anything for a fever, though...but I'm not worried, not unless it worsens. Fever's your body fighting," they said. "I need to ready myself and then we'll be on our way."

Hiram nodded, and they headed for the door, then paused after a step and turned back to Hiram. Phaedrus put a hand on his cheek and said, "It's not bad. You're going to be fine. You can trust me."

Hiram nodded. "I do."

The creature kissed him, then left.

They missed the coach they had meant to take but took the next one; Phaedrus abandoned their false slumber that day and checked Hiram's forehead about every half hour.

"Do you feel worse?" they asked.

Hiram shook his head.

"Is he sick?" a man in his forties with graying hair asked.

"It's not contagious," Phaedrus said without looking at him.

"And what about you?" he asked.

Phaedrus took a deep breath and closed their eyes. Through gritted teeth, they said, "No, I'm not contagious either."

"You are *green*. You must understand that it's unusual," the man said, taking offense at the creature's reaction.

"No, I hadn't noticed," the creature said. "Where I come from, everyone is green."

Hiram bit his lip to keep back a smile.

"And where is that?" the man asked, disgruntled now.

"Copper mines of the Atacama Desert," they said. "Leeches into the water. Happens with silver mines too, but it turns you blue."

The man cleared his throat and said nothing more.

"And you, stop smiling," Phaedrus said to Hiram.

"I'm sorry," he said.

"Yes, well, you should have seen the way people acted when I had wings," they said softly, mostly to themself.

"Wings!" Hiram exclaimed quietly.

"I worked for Thoth for a while. He gave me ibis wings," they said. "I liked them."

"What happened to them?"

"Along came a pharaoh who did *not* like the stories I told," they said. "Being still young and overly proud, I continued to tell them anyway. Four hundred years in that temple and some upstart pharaoh trying to tell me what to do!"

"The god took your wings back?"

Phaedrus shook their head. "No, the pharaoh took my wings."

"He *took* them?"

Phaedrus nodded.

"Goodness," Hiram said quietly.

"You look sweaty," they said and touched his forehead again. "Hmm."

"Hmm what?"

"You are sweaty," they said.

"Oh."

That night, the creature washed his wound again, then reapplied honey and clean bandages, muttering the whole time that Hiram should have taken better care of his arm.

Hiram didn't argue, knowing they were right; he should have, but he did not like looking at the stump or touching it. He did not like having Phaedrus look at or touch it either, though they did not seem to mind.

"Is it always going to be so ugly?" he asked while the demon wrapped his arm in bandages.

"Hiram, it is part of you," they said. "You cannot think it's ugly."

"But it is."

Phaedrus shook their head. "You must not let yourself fall into that mindset. Do not begin to hate your own body."

Hiram shrugged.

The creature took his face in their hands and urged, "Don't. Love yourself, every part. It hurts too much to do otherwise."

Hiram blinked.

"It is very hard to unlearn that sort of hatred. It stays with you, buried deep. Don't let it take root," they said and kissed his forehead. They released his face. "Still warm."

"You said you weren't worried about the fever."

"I'm not. I just wish it would go away," they said and finished wrapping his arm.

Hiram looked at the bandages. "Phaedrus?"

"Yes?"

"You don't think you're ugly, do you?" he asked.

"No," they said. "I refuse to think that."

"I don't think you're ugly either," he said and then felt immediately stupid.

Phaedrus smiled, then laughed. "I didn't think you did," they said. "Something to eat and then bed."

"I'm not hungry. You've been making me eat all day."

"Fine, then bed," the creature said. "And tomorrow morning, a doctor. Another—"

"Delay on this godforsaken journey?" Hiram asked, smiling.

"Exactly. But well worth it."

The following morning, Phaedrus and Hiram found a doctor, who scoffed at Phaedrus' application of honey, which sent the creature grumbling. "It's not *old-fashioned*," the creature said to the doctor as he removed the stitches from Hiram's stump. "It works."

"And I suppose you believe opening an umbrella inside will cause you bad luck," the doctor said.

"Please stop arguing with him while he's working," Hiram requested through gritted teeth.

The creature crossed their arms, glanced at his arm and said, "I will return momentarily. Try not to squirm too much."

Hiram wished they had not left and wished even harder when the doctor said, "Don't let your wife talk you into any more of these superstitious remedies."

"Oh...I...no..." Hiram managed.

"Women and their foolishness," he said.

Hiram coughed.

"Have you been coughing?"

"No, um, a little thirsty, I believe."

The doctor nodded, and by the time he finished removing the stitches and rewrapping the wounds, Phaedrus returned, putting a hand on his forehead and saying nothing to either of them. They paid the bill and walked out, not waiting for Hiram.

Hiram bid the doctor a hasty farewell and caught up with the creature. Hoping to make them smile, he said, "He thought you were my wife."

Phaedrus glanced at him. "I haven't been anyone's wife for centuries."

Hiram frowned. "It isn't my business, but..."

"I spent a period of time attempting to live as a woman," they said, "And as a man. I found neither of them to be...correct. For me."

"I understand," Hiram said.

"No, you don't, but you're trying. I appreciate that."

"But it does make sense," Hiram said.

Phaedrus smiled at him and went to touch Hiram's forehead again.

Hiram stepped back and said, "Phaedrus, you're fretting."

"I am allowed to fret," they said.

"It seems you think that you are allowed to do whatever you want."

The creature smiled at him. "Am I not?"

"I'm not going to try to stop you," he said.

Phaedrus' smile widened. "Take care of that hand this time."

"What hand?" he asked.

"Don't be smart," Phaedrus said, "Take care of your *stump*."

"Ugh, I wish we had another word for it."

"Arm?"

Hiram nodded.

"Then take care of your arm," they said and put a hand on his shoulder.

Hiram penned another letter to his cousin, giving an estimated date of arrival and the stage at which they would end their trip.

THE TWO of them arrived in New York City on the correct date. Phaedrus grinned, squeezed Hiram's shoulder, and said, "I can't tell you how happy I am. What are you looking at?"

Hiram pointed toward a well-dressed young man holding a sign with Hiram's full name printed on it. "That's us."

Phaedrus ogled the young man for a second and whispered, "That's how they dress their servants?"

"They're very wealthy," Hiram said and headed over to the young man. "You're here for me."

"Mr. Reinhart?"

Hiram nodded.

"You and your guest may follow me," the young man said and reached out for Hiram's suitcase. "I can take that."

"Thank you," Hiram said.

He reached out for Phaedrus' as well, and the creature handed it over.

Together they followed the man to a carriage; the young man stowed their luggage and opened the door for them. The carriage began to move, and Phaedrus asked, "Did you used to have that much money?"

"The New York branch has always been somewhat

wealthier than we Southerners, but the figures are comparable. Or...were comparable," Hiram said.

"Maybe choosing does count for something," Phaedrus said to themself. "Have you been to New York before?"

"No. Until I moved to Pickering, I spent my entire life in Georgia."

Phaedrus nodded.

The carriage stopped after half an hour or so. The young man opened the door for them. "Follow me, please," he said and led them inside.

Phaedrus stared at the sizeable townhouse to which they had been brought. When they stepped inside, a tall, thin woman dressed in deep purples and grays greeted them, kissing Hiram on the cheek. Her blonde hair was pulled into a pile on top of her head, not at all like the ringlets he recalled from their childhood.

"Hiram, dear, we're so glad to see you," she said. She pulled back and asked, "Who is your friend?"

"Oh...this is Phaedrus Queen," he said. "Phaedrus, this is a cousin of mine, Mrs. Payton Reinhart."

"Very nice to meet you," she said. "Will you be staying with us as well?"

"I would like that very much," Phaedrus said.

"Wonderful! Mason will put your things in your rooms for you," she said. She looked at Hiram's arm, pursed her lips for a moment, but said nothing. "Freshen up, then we will catch up over dinner. Ian will be home in several hours." She glanced at Phaedrus. "One of the servants can certainly bring you something earlier if you're hungry."

"Thank you, Payton," Hiram said, "You're very generous."

"Oh, your father had us to Fall's Hill so many times, it would be criminal not to return the favor," she said.

She looked at the young man who had brought them in and said, "Mason, show them upstairs."

"Yes, Mrs. Reinhart," the young man said and brought them to their rooms on the second floor.

Everything from the wallpaper to the carpet oozed luxury

and comfort. Hiram missed Fall's Hill with a sudden twist of nostalgia. The price had been brutal, paid for in the blood of hundreds of slaves, but his home had been beautiful.

"Mr. Reinhart, this will be your room. We have someone preparing a room for your friend as well."

"That's not necessary," Phaedrus said.

Mason blinked. "Are you...You are staying with us, correct?"

"Mr. Reinhart and I can share a room. No need to trouble yourself preparing another."

Mason glanced subtly at Hiram, who nodded. "Of course, whatever you wish. Let us know if you change your mind." Mason gave a small bow, then left.

"Seemed too easy," the creature noted as they entered the room together.

"Payton and Ian have...considerably fewer boundaries in their relationship than most husbands and wives," Hiram explained.

Phaedrus nodded, didn't ask for supplementary details, and explored the room, running their hands over the bedcover, touching the curtains and then finally opening a door and exclaiming, "Hiram!"

"What?"

"Come look at this bathroom," they said as they stepped through the door.

Hiram looked inside the room to see that it was elegantly furnished with a large bathtub.

The creature wasted no time turning the water on and then came back over to Hiram and untucked his shirt.

Hiram's heart surged. "Phaedrus..."

"What?" they asked, their hands still undoing his clothing.

"It's only that..."

The creature paused, then stepped back. "Too fast. I knew I would move this too quickly."

"No," Hiram said, shaking his head.

"I wasn't...I didn't intend...A bath, Hiram, I would like to take a bath with you. I won't do anything else to you."

To me? Hiram almost echoed. Instead, he said, "It's not your intentions that I'm worried about. But you did promise me that I wouldn't see you undressed."

"I trust that you'll close your eyes when I ask you to," they said. "You will, won't you?"

Hiram nodded. "Of course."

Phaedrus smiled and kissed him. "You're so good, Hiram. Out of these clothes, let's go."

Hiram undressed and slipped into the tub when Phaedrus gave him a push towards it; the creature had sprinkled shaved soap into the water, creating a thick layer of bubbles.

"Eyes closed," they said.

Hiram closed his eyes, his heart in his throat, full to the brim with excited nervousness. He sat up a little straighter when he heard Phaedrus entering the water and let out a startled breath when they touched his arm.

"You can open your eyes now."

He did and saw Phaedrus with their hair messily knotted atop their head and up to their chest in bubbles, as was Hiram.

"You look worried," they said.

"Nervous."

"About what?"

"I don't know," he said, starting to smile. "I honestly don't...it's just...I mean, Phaedrus, you're...we *are* undressed."

"You're very smart."

"I've never been undressed with anyone. It's exciting. For me, anyway."

"Nothing new for me," Phaedrus said, smiling confidently for a second, then looking away.

"You say things like that a lot."

"Like what?"

"Like you're bragging, but you sound regretful."

Phaedrus bit their lip for a moment, then explained, "I don't mean to imply that I am ashamed of the things I've done, but I wonder if I should be. I've taken a variety of lovers over my life, with mixed results, clearly. I wonder if the blame for that is mine."

Hiram shook his head. "I don't believe so."

"Of course you don't," they said. "I don't think so either, but it's...when everyone around you becomes concerned with purity and virtue, self-reflection is inevitable."

"I can't say I've thought about it much."

"No?"

Hiram shrugged. "My father didn't care for things like purity or virtue. I don't know what my mother cared about, not really."

"What did your father care for?"

"Power, fear, cruelty."

"So how did you turn out so sweet?" Phaedrus asked.

Hiram thought. "He turned me over to be raised by slaves, even more so after my mother passed. He taught me magic and tried to teach me to be a man, but Susan and Cassie taught me...well, almost everything else. They brought me to bed each night and bathed me and fed me and soothed me when I became upset. They became my world, and he hurt them, awfully and frequently. I realized quickly that I never wanted to be like him."

Phaedrus studied him, clearly disturbed by what Hiram had shared.

He felt the need to add, "Plantations are hideous places. My story isn't uncommon."

"No, not uncommon at all. Slavery has always been an ugly mark on human history. Never quite like this, but present and unbecoming," the creature said. "But how you chose to deal with your circumstances was unusual."

Hiram sighed.

"Thank you for sharing with me."

He nodded. He wanted to think about something else. Something other than his dead parents and the vicious cruelty of plantation life and the dire consequences it had had for the women, and the girl, he loved.

"Once," Phaedrus began without warning, "near the foot

of the Zagros Mountains lived a very poor man and his wife."

The break in the dolorous silence between them took Hiram unaware. He sat up a little straighter.

"They had nothing in their small house and rarely enough to fill their bellies. They conceived a son, and the wife gave birth one night. They fretted, for they had nothing with which to wrap their child. Not a scrap of cloth or bit of wool. They fretted and the father cried, 'He may die by morning!' A man came to them that very night and said, 'Peace be upon you. Please, have you any straw? My wife has just given birth and the child may die of cold without anything for us to lay him upon.' The couple answered, 'We are very poor, but we have straw. You may take as much as you need for your child'. The man filled up his cloak with straw and left..."

Hiram relaxed, soothed by the softness of their voice, but drawn in by it as well. When they finished, he smiled lazily at them.

"Aren't you going to say you liked my story?" Phaedrus prompted lightheartedly.

"Turn around," Hiram said instead. "Please."

"I almost liked that better without the please," Phaedrus said and turned around.

Hiram leaned forward and put his arms around Phaedrus, pulling them back so that they were chest to back. He placed a kiss on Phaedrus' shoulder, then settled against the side of the tub. "I liked your story."

Phaedrus leaned back against him. "This is a lovely tub," they sighed, eyes closed.

"It is nice to be rich," Hiram said.

"Nice soap, too," they said.

"Mhm," Hiram said. He ran his hand along the creature's side and stomach, finding an easy, comfortable layer of fat over their belly. He found himself wanting to rest his cheek against that small, soft stomach.

"It all goes right there, every sweet and savory morsel," they said and placed one of their hands over his. "Well, most of it."

"Oh?" Hiram asked, not sure what else to say.

"Some goes here," they said and moved his hand down to caress their thigh. They guided his hand to their inner thigh. "Especially here."

Hiram swallowed and took a deep breath.

"Something wrong?" they asked.

"No, I...I don't want to do anything you don't want me to."

"So then ask what you are allowed to do," Phaedrus instructed. They released his hand and arched their back to press against him.

"Can I touch you?" he asked.

"I want to let you," they said, "Very much."

"But then I would know. Or at least have an idea, I suppose."

Phaedrus pulled away from him and turned around. They regarded Hiram seriously. "Promise me that I'm more than what you'll find between my legs."

"I promise."

They looked into his eyes and finally professed, "I believe you." They smiled. "I really do."

Phaedrus leaned in and kissed him, sliding onto his lap, sending the water sloshing in the tub. They opened their mouth against his again, which caused Hiram's heart to patter anxiously but delightfully in his chest.

Hiram wrapped his handless arm around their waist to bring them closer and returned his other hand to their thigh, squeezing gently. Covered in bubbles and unable to see exactly what he was doing, Hiram reached out to touch them between the legs and grinned when the creature let out a trembling sigh. The sigh was followed by a slow moan and other sounds of pleasure. As Hiram struck a balance between exploration and caressing, Phaedrus pressed closer to him, moving their hips in time with his hand, their face buried in his neck.

With their eyes shut and their hands gripping his sides, the demon bit him tenderly, causing Hiram to gasp.

"Too hard?" they asked.

"No," he breathed.

Phaedrus moved one hand from Hiram's side to between his legs, stroking him, and returned their mouth to his. A rush moved through him after several minutes and his breath caught in his throat until he spilled over the creature's hand.

The demon pleaded, "Faster, please, I'm…"

Hiram heeded the request, fumbling and nervous, but he hoped also pleasingly eager.

The creature cried out, shaking a little. They put one of their hands over his to stop him from moving. "Enough," they breathed.

He stopped.

"Did you…?" Hiram asked when they had been still for a moment. They had sounded satisfied, and Hiram suspected, but did not know for sure, that they had finished.

"Yes, Hiram," they said patiently. They peered over the side of the tub. "Oh, we've made a mess. Next time on the bed, then."

"Of course," Hiram agreed vapidly.

"Come help me clean up. We'd be terrible guests otherwise."

"Not yet," he said and tightened his arms around them. He couldn't stand the idea of being without them in his arms just yet. He wondered if they always pulled away so fast after something intimate. Maybe they still doubted him or regretted what they'd done.

Maybe, Hiram hoped, they simply abhorred being a bad houseguest. That he understood.

Phaedrus returned his embrace and kissed his forehead. "I hope your fever's not coming back."

"No, I just…I'm warm all over."

They lingered together for a little while, then Phaedrus stood and reached for a towel while Hiram stared after them. They glanced back.

Hiram looked away. "I'm sorry."

"No, you're all right," they assured him with a wave of one broad but delicate hand. "After that, I expect you know what you're dealing with."

"If I say no, will you think me stupid?"

Phaedrus snorted and wrapped the towel around themself. "I'll try to remember your inexperience before saying something so cruel. Couldn't you tell?"

Hiram couldn't keep his eyes from darting over Phaedrus' body. He knew what he'd touched and knew why Phaedrus would expect him to make assumptions. He shrugged. "I'll be more studious next time."

"Next time," Phaedrus muttered.

"I've always been quite studious," Hiram informed them. "Give me half a chance, and I'll make for a very eager pupil."

"Mr. Reinhart, I think you might be a bit of a rascal." The creature held out a towel to him.

He stood to take it, drying himself. "As long as you don't find it unbecoming."

"Not at all." They put a hand on his waist and leaned to rest their forehead on his shoulder. Softly, they nearly begged, "You think of me the same as you did before. Tell me you do."

"I promised, didn't I?"

Phaedrus let out a small sigh.

Hiram assured them, "You've told me what you aren't. How foolish would I have to be to doubt you?"

They swallowed. "I cannot help but doubt."

"Imagine I'd lived my whole life in a world where I haven't eaten anything but...but bread and meat. Rye and barley, pork and chicken, but just bread and meat, no matter the varieties. Never seen a pumpkin or an apple in my life. No idea what a huckleberry or a squash is. And imagine one day, someone asks me, 'Hiram, would you care for a strawberry?'"

"Are you going to eat me?" Phaedrus asked.

"Imagine what a fool I would be to look at a strawberry and think, 'Ah, yes, this must be a crumpet, or perhaps some sort of lamb.'"

"There are quite a few flaws in this metaphor," Phaedrus pointed out.

"I regret to inform you that it's the very best I can do to

express my understanding of the matter at present." Hiram slid his fingers along their jaw. "I can attempt to do better, but I don't think there's any point to continuous efforts to rehash what you've already explained perfectly well."

"Perfectly well?" Phaedrus echoed.

"Absolutely clearly. And insistently. And *repeatedly*," Hiram teased gently.

They smiled at his teasing. "This could be something, Hiram. As long as we make it, this could work out beautifully."

"I hope so," Hiram said, putting an arm around them.

"And if we don't, then I'm glad to have had this time with you."

"I have faith that this plan will work, I really do."

"Good," they said and kissed him one last time before walking away.

As they did, Hiram noticed a pair of markings on their shoulder blades, identical in shape and form: two slightly jagged lines about eight inches long.

"On your back," he began and didn't continue, not knowing if it would be impolite.

"Wings, yes," they said. "All the other Fallen think it's hilarious—an angel who's really lost their wings."

Hiram eyed the scars a moment longer, noting that they had the texture and mild sheen of scars left by magic, not by weapons.

The creature gathered up towels and handed one to Hiram, pointing to the water on the floor. The soaked up what they could and drained the tub in an attempt not to be terrible guests. After that, they dressed and Hiram asked, "Where do you get your clothes?"

"The same place a great deal of people do—a tailor."

Hiram frowned and looked around for his shirt.

Phaedrus shrugged. "I don't know what you wanted me to say. If you wanted to know why I wear what I do instead of what you do, that is a different question. Stop."

Hiram stopped and asked, "What?"

"Change your bandages. Are you *trying* to get sick? They're soaked."

"It's difficult to do with one hand."

"So ask for help."

Hiram sighed and looked away. He began to unwind the wet bandages.

"Hiram, ask if you want help," the creature said.

"I'll manage."

The creature huffed.

Hiram tossed aside the bandages and dried off his arm. He examined it for signs of health, ill or good, and decided that it looked as it should. He rummaged through his things for the extra bandages Phaedrus had purchased but couldn't find them. He sighed.

"They're in my bag," the creature said from their seat on the bed.

"May I have them?"

The creature nodded and retrieved the bandages. They held them out for Hiram to take but pulled them back before he could. "Maybe you ought to let it air for a little while."

He acquiesced, sitting on the bed.

"You've got something on your face, right here," they said, tapping their cheek.

Hiram brushed his cheek off.

"No, here," they said and reached over. "Make a wish," they said, holding out the eyelash on a single finger.

Hiram blew and made his wish.

"The hand didn't grow back," they teased.

It took Hiram a moment to understand, but then he said, "That's not what I'd wish for."

"I didn't think so," they said and looked around, then took up a hairbrush. They began to brush their hair, frowning at the ends. "Do you think I should cut it?"

"It's your hair."

"No, stupid, look at the ends," they said. "They're starting to get frazzled."

"Oh. I suppose, then, if you think it will help," he said.

They rolled their eyes.

Hiram lay down on the bed, still without a shirt, and looked up at the ceiling. He closed his eyes after a moment, trying to think of something pleasant and not dwell on his possibly impending death.

"Do you truly believe June will get in trouble for warning me?"

"Certainly."

He opened his eyes. "A lot of trouble?"

"Unpleasant more than terrible, I assume, unless he's been breaking a lot of rules," Phaedrus said. "He must like you if he's keeping an eye on your grave from the future."

"He came for Christmas one time but got told off for it. That...oh, I forget what he called them..."

"The Temporal Parliament."

"That."

"They do not approve of anything but linear movement through time. My king has a lot of spats with them," they said. "Of course, it's all bluster and bad moods when they're dealing with him. There's only one being that can make him do what he doesn't want to do."

"God."

"I imagine Him too, but I meant his wife," they said, "And she isn't much for telling others what to do."

"I see."

Phaedrus reached out and traced along his chest with a finger. "I think I know what I want to do with you next."

An unfamiliar buzz went through Hiram and settled in his stomach, a mixture of apprehension and eagerness. "You do?" he asked, embarrassed when his voice caught in his throat.

They grinned. "I do."

"Can I ask?"

They shook their head. "Not yet." They leaned forward and kissed him. "What do you think we'll have for dinner? I hope it's something nice."

"It will be."

"Good."

They braided their hair and pulled it over one shoulder, then lay down beside Hiram. "Do you feel sleepy?"

"Somewhat, yes."

They nestled close to him. "Do you have dreams, Hiram?"

"Sometimes. There's this one where I'm outside, and I think it's a forest—"

"I meant aspirations," they clarified.

"Oh. Yes, though they aren't very grand."

"That's good, neither are mine," they said.

Hiram adjusted himself so that he had an arm around the creature and their head rested on his shoulder. "I'd like for Ellen to go to a good school when she's older, though I worry that her race may preclude that."

"There is always Europe."

"She has expressed an interest in magic. I wonder if the university in Triviai would serve her well," he said, "Though there is the matter of paying tuition."

"I believe they have a very good scholarship program for young ladies," Phaedrus said, "Or they did when last I was there. They hold the education of women highly there."

"Do they?"

"It has to do with the king's mother. Quite the spitfire, I've heard."

"He never mentioned," Hiram said.

"What?"

He clarified, "Ashley, he never mentioned his mother."

"On a first-name basis with the king of Triviai?" they asked.

"His request."

"You know him?"

"We met once, a few years ago," Hiram said, "When I stole twenty-nine people."

Phaedrus sat up, propping themself up on an elbow, and said, "The more you mention it, the more it sounds like an interesting story."

"A very daring adventure," he said flatly.

"Tell me, Hiram."

Hiram sat up and sighed, reaching for his shirt.

"What are you doing?"

"I didn't know I had to be shirtless to tell the tale," he said, pulling it on and starting to button it.

The creature reached over and helped him. "All set, now tell me."

Hiram grinned, settled against the headboard and began the story of how he had ended up fleeing to Canada with a number of stolen slaves.

AT DINNER, Payton introduced them to her husband, a man with reddish-blond hair and gray eyes, saying "Hiram, dear, have you met Ian?"

"No, I haven't had the pleasure," he said.

She said, "Ian's heard all about Fall's Hill and our little adventures."

"Very pleased to meet you," Ian said, shaking Hiram's hand and glancing at Phaedrus.

Hiram gestured to the creature and said, "This is Phaedrus Queen, malak ha-satan, among the first fallen."

"Goodness, what a title," Payton said to herself.

"Pleased to meet you as well," Ian said, shaking Phaedrus' hand more delicately than he had shaken Hiram's and making eye contact in a way that nearly made Hiram frown.

Phaedrus nodded their head and extracted their hand.

"Come, sit," Payton said.

They all sat, with Ian at the head of the table and Phaedrus seated to his right. They chatted pleasantly as they waited for their courses. Ian continued to eye the demon, and Phaedrus in response emptied their glass of wine faster than the others and accepted another each time a server offered one.

Hiram glanced at them, and Phaedrus wrinkled their nose at him.

"So, Hiram, you haven't said what brings you to New York," Payton said as she took up a spoon to eat the sorbet in front of her.

"I was hoping to ask for a favor," Hiram said.

"Oh?" she said, pretending very well that she had not expected him to ask for something. "A favor in what amount?"

"It's not money," he clarified.

"Really?" Ian asked.

"Surprising, I know," he said. "I'd like to borrow your Germanic long-form script dictionary."

Payton blinked; it was an odd but unexciting thing to want to borrow. "Oh."

"We need it to set a trap," Phaedrus said, peering into their wine glass and glancing around for a servant.

Hiram leaned over and took the glass from them and set it in front of his own plate. "Try the sorbet," he suggested.

"What sort of trap?" Ian asked.

"I need to locate another mage," he said.

"You're being stingy with the details," Payton scolded.

Hiram said, "It isn't terribly interesting."

"A man named Blackwell wants to kill me for making off with his wife," Phaedrus said, "and we've lost track of him."

"With his wife?" Ian asked, sounding interested.

"Not like that," Phaedrus said.

"But for what do you need the dictionary?" Payton asked.

"To bait the trap," Phaedrus amended.

"Blackwell wants it," Hiram said. "I'd like to borrow it and put it up for auction at Oswald Lysander's."

"It is where you go to look for things," Ian agreed.

"I hope it isn't asking too much," Hiram addressed his cousin.

"No, certainly not," she said.

"Good. I'm not ready to die, not at his hands," Phaedrus said and reached over to take their glass back from where

Hiram had placed it.

Hiram put out a hand to stop them from taking it back and in a low voice asked, "Don't you think you've had enough?"

"No."

"Phaedrus, please," he said softly.

The demon leaned in a little bit and whispered into Hiram's ear, "Either you let me drink or you tell our host to stop checking my trouser front to see if I've got a cock or not."

Hiram glanced at Ian without meaning to, released the creature's hand, and said, "Fine, then, as you were."

"Sharing secrets?" Payton asked pleasantly.

"Just a little one," Phaedrus said.

Hiram cleared his throat. "I hope it isn't imposing to ask to borrow the dictionary."

"No, of course not! We're a little lacking in adventure right now. I'm glad to help," assured Payton.

"Thank you. It means everything that we do this," Hiram said.

Payton pushed another bit of food around her plate. "First thing in the morning."

"Thank you," Phaedrus said.

They chatted a little while after dessert. Ian asked Phaedrus a lot of personal questions, wanting to know the meaning of their title and why their skin had 'such an interesting hue.'

"And you're the sort of man who likes interesting things, aren't you?" Phaedrus asked, rolling their half-full wine glass along their lip.

"I am," Ian said, making eye contact with the demon.

Hiram rubbed his nose and glanced at Payton, who was watching Ian with an amused smile.

Phaedrus let out a breath through their nose. "Of course. Always the rich ones."

"You look...um, you look like you might want to lie down," Hiram advised softly.

"I *do* want to lie down," Phaedrus agreed abruptly,

standing up.

Ian stood as well, offering the creature a hand. "I can walk you to your room."

Hiram stood, a sick feeling settling over him.

"No, Hiram, stay and catch up with Payton," Ian offered, putting a hand on Phaedrus' elbow.

"No, thank you, Ian. I think I might also retire. We've done a lot of traveling recently..." Hiram said, looking at the demon, who didn't seem distressed.

Phaedrus held out a hand to Hiram. "We'll go to bed."

Hiram took their hand, and the creature pulled him along, moving away from Ian, saying, "Just us, though, not you, Ian. Just me and Hiram. Hiram and I? I don't know."

The mage glanced back and saw that Ian had crossed his arms and started to frown.

Hiram put a hand on the creature's arm and steered them toward their room while Phaedrus said, "But I bet he's got a lot of nice things to steal. That wouldn't be so bad. It's been a long time since I've stolen something nice. I mean *really* nice, can't-walk-by-it nice."

"That is entirely up to you," Hiram said, "but it might be best if you wait until after we get what we need from them. We wouldn't want to risk their help."

"Maybe you're right," the demon conceded.

Once in the room, Phaedrus flopped onto the bed, trying to tug Hiram with them.

Hiram pulled back and asked, "Do you want me to find another place to sleep?"

"No. Why would I want that?"

"Because you're drunk," Hiram said, sounding snottier than he intended.

"And we disapprove, don't we, Mr. Reinhart?" the creature asked, not turning to look at him and pulling a pillow into their arms.

"I didn't say that."

"Then are we jealous?" they asked.

"No."

"Envious?"

"I just said I wasn't."

"Jealous and envious are *different*."

Hiram walked away, going to the bathroom to clean his teeth and wash his face. He changed and climbed under the covers, turning his back to Phaedrus.

"Hiram?"

He didn't respond.

"Hiram, you're not angry, are you?"

"No."

The creature reached over and shook him. "*Hiram.*"

"I'm not angry. You should get ready for bed," he said.

Phaedrus got out of bed, and Hiram heard them moving around the room, turning on the water in the bathroom and muttering to themself. When they returned to bed, they lay still and silent on their side of the bed.

Hiram sighed and rolled over. He nudged Phaedrus with his head. "I'm not upset with you. I don't like the way Ian behaved toward you."

Phaedrus nestled into him. "No, me neither."

Hiram put an arm around the creature's waist. "Goodnight, Phaedrus."

"Goodnight, Hiram."

In the morning Phaedrus woke him up, shaking him gently at first, then more urgently. "Hiram."

"What?"

"Wake up, we have to go to that...the auction house you mentioned, I can't recall the name."

Hiram sat up and rubbed his face.

Phaedrus grinned at him.

"What?"

"Your hair's gone all wild," the creature said.

He reached up to touch it.

Phaedrus continued to grin. "We should get ready."

Hiram nodded and moved toward the edge of the bed, but Phaedrus grabbed him by the arm. "What?"

"We do have a little time."

Hiram glanced toward the window and saw only pale light coming through. "What time is it, Phaedrus?"

"I couldn't sleep," the creature confessed. "I mean, I did sleep, but then I woke up, and I couldn't get back to sleep."

He lay back down and buried his face in the pillow.

The demon remained upright and said, "I have to confess, Hiram, I'm worried about that man."

"Blackwell?"

"Ian."

"Oh. Yes."

"That he's still...we are clearly together, are we not, Hiram?"

He looked up, unsure of what to say. "I..."

"Given that being together exclusively *is* your intention," Phaedrus said, "I had assumed you wanted something more than a casual affair."

"I do."

Phaedrus began to play with their hair, taking it out from the braid they kept it in at night. "Would it be unwise, then, for one of us to tell Ian that his interest would intrude on our relationship?"

"Would you like me to speak to him?" Hiram asked.

They nodded, their face tight with worry, and said, "I would. Very much."

"Then—"

"But do you worry that it would distance them from our cause?"

"If it does, we will find another way," the mage said.

The demon gave a small smile that did not look happy.

Hiram sat up and put his arms around the creature. "Besides, it is Payton's help we require, not Ian's, and I know that she is not petty."

Phaedrus returned his embrace and nestled their face against his chest; they remained together like that for a while, quiet and concerned with what would come.

"I would like to take a bath," Phaedrus said, "with you."

"I have no objections to that."

"But a real bath, with washing, not with...uh...more intimate things," they said.

"I remain objection-less," Hiram said.

"I thought you might," Phaedrus said, moving out of his arms and standing. They stretched and said, "But then again, I've had my suspicions about you since the start."

"What suspicions are those?"

"That you might be genuinely kind and good," Phaedrus said.

"I try," Hiram said, unable to stop a silly grin from spreading across his face. "But if you thought that..."

"Why did I delay things between us? Because kind and good people cannot always, umm, appreciate or comprehend that I am not one thing or the other."

Hiram nodded and wondered what Phaedrus had been like in centuries past, what they had looked like long ago, in the times when they had attempted to be something other than what they were. It didn't feel right to wonder what they had looked like trying to be a man or a woman and he tried to think of something else.

"Stop looking at me like that," the creature warned.

Hiram looked away. "I'm sorry."

Phaedrus said nothing and walked towards the bathroom.

Hiram wondered if he had been uninvited from their bath; there was no way they could have known, but he felt that they must, from the clipped tone they had taken. He stood and tentatively approached the bathroom, tapping the door with his knuckles.

"Come in," they said.

He entered.

"What's that kicked dog look for, Hiram?" they asked, setting down their toothbrush.

"I'm sorry."

"Don't be dramatic."

"I shouldn't have—"

"Stop," Phaedrus said. "It was a look and that was it. I asked you to stop, and you did. It is done."

"I wondered, though, about...about you. What you would have been like...you said you were someone's wife once..." he said, not sure how to admit his guilt, not wanting to apply either term to the creature out loud. "I wondered what you were like as...that."

"And has it changed anything? How you feel about me?"

"No. Of course not."

"Then I am not concerned. To be honest, I'm not entirely pleased, but I don't think you'd be pleased about the things I've wondered about you," they said. "Clean your teeth and get ready for a bath."

Phaedrus walked out of the bathroom, closing the door as they left, and returned only when Hiram had reopened the door.

"What things have you wondered about me?" Hiram asked.

"They are not entirely flattering," the demon said, "It might be best not to share."

"Maybe."

Phaedrus turned on the water and began to shed their clothes.

Hiram followed their example and caught the creature looking at him several times.

"You're mostly legs, aren't you?" they asked.

Hiram glanced down at his body. "I don't think so."

"And arms; you're all limbs, Hiram," they said, testing the water then climbing in. They held out a hand.

Hiram took their hand and climbed in, settling into their arms for a moment.

They kissed his forehead and said, "Hand me the soap."

Hiram obeyed and tried his best to keep from wiggling too much while Phaedrus washed him, though they seemed to make no effort to keep their hands from straying to a tender or ticklish spot.

By the time they had both finished, Hiram could hear other people stirring in the house. He watched Phaedrus begin to comb their hair and asked, "You'll be a while with that, right?"

"Yes."

"I'll be back."

They continued to comb their hair as he dressed. He left the room and encountered one of the servants, Mason, looking rumpled and sleepy. Upon seeing Hiram, Mason straightened himself and his clothing and said, "Good morning, Mr. Reinhart. Is there something you needed?"

"Are my cousins awake?" he asked.

"Yes," said the young man, then his cheeks turned red and he added, "I believe so, anyway. I haven't been in."

Hiram raised an eyebrow but said nothing; he seemed embarrassed enough as it was. "Thank you," he said and headed toward his cousins' room.

"Um, sir..." Mason said.

He glanced back.

"Make sure you knock."

Hiram nodded and continued. He knocked on their door and Payton called for him to enter. He found her in a robe, leaning against the doorframe of their bathroom, which looked to be twice the size of the one in the guest room.

"Something you needed?" she asked. "Come in all the way, Hiram, I won't bite."

He entered the room farther and closed the door behind himself. "I'd like to speak with Ian if it's not too early."

She glanced toward the bed, where Ian lay face down, burrowed in pillows and blankets. "About your friend?" she asked.

He nodded.

"Ian, get up. Hiram wants to speak with you," she said.

Ian stirred, then sat up, the blankets moving away to reveal pink marks and bruises on his skin. Hiram stared and glanced towards his cousin, but she had already gone into the bathroom, closing the door. He heard the water turn on.

Ian turned to face him, arranging the blankets on his lap. "Hiram?"

"It's about Phaedrus."

The man smiled. "What about him?" he asked. "Her?"

"Them."

"Do you know?" he asked. "I mean, Mason says you two are sharing a room. You must know."

"They're not interested. In you, in whatever you and Payton have going on."

"She likes to watch—"

"I didn't ask, and I don't care," Hiram interrupted. "I came to ask you to leave them alone."

Ian regarded him for a moment, his gray eyes clouded with thought and a degree of hurt. "We have a little fun, that's all. No one gets hurt, not unless they want to."

"Ian, it's not about that. It's not about you," Hiram said. "It's about us."

Ian shrugged and said, sounding pouty, "Fine."

Hiram nodded and headed for the door, but turned back and said, "And don't ever ask about that again. About being a man or a woman or what they've got beneath their clothes."

The other man frowned.

"I mean it," the mage said, feeling warm.

Ian nodded. "I was curious. That isn't a crime."

"It's hurtful, though," Hiram said.

"Oh," Ian said, his eyes widening a little. "I didn't think...I certainly didn't mean to be unkind."

"No, I don't think you did, but you did it anyway," Hiram said. Ian did not seem to be a cruel person. Hiram regarded him for a moment, wondering his age and where Payton had found him. "Are you from New York?"

"Not the city, no," he said. "My family lives near the Finger Lakes. Cayuga, if you want to get exact."

Hiram could not have named a single Finger Lake under the best of circumstances, let alone in this one. "Are you a Reinhart?" he asked, wondering if Payton had elected to break with family tradition and marry someone who wasn't a cousin.

He nodded. "On my father's side only. My mother, uh, she was a milkmaid," he confessed with an uncomfortable note in his voice.

Hiram nodded. "That's good, though. New blood helps."

"That's what my father says," Ian said. "Payton says that...no, never mind."

"What?"

"That your fathers wanted the two of you to be married."

Hiram smiled. "Luckily for both of us, my father died," he said, recalling the now-extinct dread that had always accompanied Payton's visits and his father's assurances that she would make a good planter's wife.

"A slave killed him," Ian said.

"His son killed him," Hiram corrected. "Joshua."

"Oh," Ian said, eyes wide. "I didn't imagine..."

"If you want to hear about something truly debauched, I'll tell you what happens on plantations," Hiram said. "It will make having your servant boy spank you seem very tame."

Ian turned bright red.

Hiram laughed. "I'll see you at breakfast." He left, returning to the room he shared with Phaedrus.

They had dressed and sat on the bed, legs crossed, waiting. "You spoke with him?"

Hiram nodded. "He'll leave you alone."

"Will he really?"

"I don't think Ian is as..."

"Decadent?" Phaedrus supplied.

"Mm, as he tries to seem. I think he's fallen into the glamourous idealization of excess, but he's harmless."

"All that from ten minutes?"

Hiram nodded. "People are easier to read when they've just woken up and don't have any clothes on."

"Oh, I see," Phaedrus said, giving Hiram a suspicious look.

"He still had blankets on if you're worried."

"No," Phaedrus said.

Hiram believed them.

They stood, stretched and went over to Hiram, putting their arms around him. "Can we stay like this forever?"

"If that's what you want."

"No," they said. "I want to take you out to a little house in the country and put flowers in your hair and fatten you up."

Hiram smiled. "It will never happen."

"You don't like flowers?"

"I'll never be fat," he said.

Phaedrus giggled and kissed him. "I'll find a way, get you proper roly-poly."

Hiram smiled and hugged them tightly.

HIRAM, PHAEDRUS, Payton, and Ian arrived at Oswald Lysander's place of business late in the morning, around ten-thirty. Lysander ran his business out of a remodeled townhouse in lower Manhattan.

Ian and Phaedrus brushed against each other as they entered the building behind the other two. Hiram heard Phaedrus say, "Oh, excuse me."

Sounding mortified, Ian said, "I'm so sorry. It was an accident, I promise."

Hiram glanced backward.

Phaedrus scolded, "Hiram, what did you do to the poor thing?"

"I didn't do anything to him," Hiram said.

Ian looked nervous and red about the face.

Hiram glanced at his cousin, who shook her head.

"I may have eavesdropped on your conversation, but I didn't do anything to reinforce it," she said.

"It's...I didn't mean to say something that would be hurtful," Ian said in a rush, "And I shouldn't have been overly forward with you, but I didn't...I didn't imagine...! I didn't think. I never do."

Phaedrus patted Ian on the arm. "You'll do better, I'm sure. The important thing about mistakes is that we learn from them."

Ian smiled anxiously. "I will."

Phaedrus smiled at him and took their hand back. To Payton, he said, "What a nice little husband you've found."

She looked fondly at Ian. "I do care for him very much."

Ian smiled at her, then looked to the ground.

Hiram and Phaedrus traded looks.

Their party entered a parlor decorated with Oriental rugs, low tables of dark wood, and deep purple throw pillows. Phaedrus, Hiram thought, would have looked particularly at home lounging on those pillows.

"Are you here to see Mr. Lysander?" asked a neatly dressed middle-aged woman. She looked up at them from behind a desk and didn't appear to know exactly what to make of their group.

"Yes, we have an appointment," Payton said. "Under Reinhart."

The woman checked her paperwork and stood. She left the room and returned a few minutes later with a man in his mid-sixties who appeared to be of Near Eastern descent. He greeted them and invited him into his office, where they all sat with murmurs and fabric rustles.

"Now, Mr. Reinhart, what is it that you're here for?" Lysander asked.

Hiram and Ian both began to speak at the same time, then looked at each other and went quiet.

Payton informed Lysander, "We have something we'd like to put up for sale. It's a dictionary for one of those antiquated long-form scripts."

Lysander rustled through his papers for a moment, then asked, "Germanic?"

They all glanced at each other.

"I hear when people are looking for certain items. There's been a mage causing quite a stir looking for that dictionary and some other items as well."

"Like what?" Hiram asked.

"Cold iron and hard mercury, feathers from a cockerel that hatched a basilisk," Lysander said. "A few other sundry items."

Hiram glanced at Phaedrus, who frowned, their head tilted inquisitively. "I'll tell you later," he murmured.

Phaedrus nodded.

"Mr. Lysander, I'm sure you're aware of my family's standing," Payton said.

The old man nodded.

"I am hoping that we will be able to put this book up for sale under another name to lure out this buyer," she said, "We have a grievance with him."

"Do you know the name of the prospective buyer?" Lysander asked.

"Mathew Blackwell," Hiram said.

"I haven't heard the name," Lysander said.

"He is a mage of some consequence," Hiram explained, "In Canada."

"Oh, Canada," the man said a little disdainfully.

"If we can apprehend this man and solve our grievance, we would be grateful," Payton said.

Lysander said, "May I see the book?"

Ian, who had been charged with carrying the item, handed it over.

"Very nice condition. Magically preserved, I imagine," he said, mostly to himself. "It will be worth a decent amount to an interested collector. You don't want this listed under your name?"

"No," Payton said.

"An estate sale then, for the recently deceased Mr. William Cobbler," he said, "We still haven't finished the inventory for that. Your...target should buy the story readily enough."

"I imagine so. He was a renowned collector."

"I will notify you when we have a bid on your item," Lysander said.

"Thank you very much, Mr. Lysander," Payton said. "We can see ourselves out, no need to stand."

As they left, Phaedrus leaned close to Hiram and whispered, "Didn't that seem too easy?"

"Being a Reinhart makes things easy," Hiram said, "If you don't throw away a fortune and move to a frozen wasteland where your family name means nothing."

"No one made you do that, Hiram. You chose it. Stop complaining," Payton said.

"I couldn't stay there," Hiram said. "Not with the things the way they were. It was...barbaric, inhuman, the things that were done."

"I'm not saying it wasn't. I'm saying I think your way of handling it was drastic," she said. "You're a Reinhart. There's no reason for you to live as you do."

He shook his head. "You don't understand."

Payton raised an eyebrow. "Ah, yes, I always have been such a naïve girl. How could I forget my ignorance?"

"You know that's not what I meant," he sulked.

Phaedrus offered, "All you have to do is make your name mean something again."

Hiram glanced at them.

"You could do it," the demon said, "if you put your mind to it."

Hiram had not thought of rising above where he'd lowered himself. He had quietly resigned himself to a life of toil and poverty. Perhaps he had accepted it as a punishment for the crimes of his family. His current family, though, had done nothing to deserve it.

Horrifically, he realized he'd seen it as their lot in life. What more could runaways hope for than impoverished freedom? What more did they deserve? Hannah and Cassie had spent all their years without a single bit of finery, and Ellen had never had more than a single dress and one rag doll.

He cursed his foolishness and narrowmindedness. His family did not deserve to wallow alongside him in his self-imposed punishment. They deserved good things for once. All the good things he could give them.

"You seem capable enough," they said.

"Thank you," he mumbled, distracted by his thoughts.

"Ian and I are going to pay a call to a friend while we're in the area," Payton said. "You may join us, of course, but you can also return home."

"I wouldn't want to intrude," Phaedrus said, "or cause a commotion."

Payton nodded. "We won't be out very long."

Hiram and Phaedrus returned to the Reinhart townhouse. The demon took him by the hand and pulled him towards their room. They brought him inside and closed the door. "Do you think it will work, Hiram? Do you think we'll be safe soon?" they asked.

"Yes."

They kissed his cheek and requested softly, "Undress for me."

Hiram swallowed and began to shed his clothes.

Once he was naked, the demon hugged him, still clothed in loose, soft fabric that brushed against Hiram's skin.

"Are you going to leave your clothes on?" Hiram asked.

"Yes," Phaedrus said. "Lay on your stomach."

Hiram hesitated for a moment, but went to the bed and lay down, nervous and excited. Phaedrus came and straddled his thighs; they leaned forward and kissed his shoulder. "You can always tell me stop, Hiram, at any time."

"Thank you," Hiram said.

"I won't, um, put anything inside you without asking, so you don't have to worry about that, either," the demon soothed. "You can relax."

Hiram bit his lip to keep in a nervous giggle. He decidedly could not relax.

The creature kissed his shoulder again and then his neck. They kissed his back, moving their lips down to touch his rear and thighs. Hiram gasped when their tongue traced along his inner thigh, moving up.

The sensation sent a strange surge through him, an

overwhelmed feeling that was almost fear. He gripped the sheets and closed his eyes, not sure if he wanted this to stop. He couldn't see what was happening, had no idea where this would go. He gasped when Phaedrus continued to move his tongue higher and said, "I..."

The creature pulled back. "Yes?"

"Can I...do I have to stay on my stomach?"

"No, of course not," they said. Their weight lifted from him.

Hiram sat up and tried not to pull away. His heart pattered fretfully.

They reached over to touch his face. "Did I worry you?"

"I've...it's that...I've never..." He swallowed.

"Shh, Hiram, you don't have to make excuses," Phaedrus assured. They put their arms around Hiram. They pulled the mage into their lap and kissed his curls. "I don't want to do anything you don't want."

"It's not that I don't want to, to, ah, try new things." Hiram felt safe and content wrapped up in their arms. His heart slowed and his breathing evened.

"I understand." They pressed their lips to his hair again.

Hiram wrapped his arms around their neck and kissed them.

"What about on your back?" they asked. "That's a little less scary."

Hiram nodded.

Phaedrus, reminding him again of their unexpected strength, lifted him out of their lap and settled him on his back. They arranged a few pillows behind his head so that he was not entirely horizontal. They kissed his stomach and then his hips, their teeth nipping a little at his skin. Being able to look down at the demon diminished the fear he had felt, leaving him only with excited anxiety, waiting tensely to find where their mouth would go next.

They ran their tongue along him and took him into their mouth, causing Hiram to sigh and close his eyes. Every so often, a piece of their clothing would rustle, or their mouth would make a small sound and that would bring Hiram back to reality, but not by much.

His hand began to hurt, an aching pain that, at first, he barely felt, too interested in other sensations. He brushed it off as nothing but phantom pains, but the ache grew, becoming agonizing.

"Something's wrong," he said, his voice panicky, unable to think of anything but the pain in his hand.

Phaedrus sat up immediately, looking concerned, almost frightened. "I'm sorry, what was it?"

"No, my hand." He turned to look at his hand but saw only the stump. A hand that wasn't there.

Phaedrus nodded. "At it again?" they asked.

"It's not the same," Hiram said. His missing hand had pained him somewhat with itching and burning before, but nothing like this. "It's...it's not right."

The creature reached over to look at his stump, touching the end with careful fingers.

Hiram flinched, the area oversensitive.

Phaedrus began to unwind the bandages and pulled back once they saw the flesh. The veins in his arm had taken a strange hue, tinting the skin closest to the end of his arm.

"Something is wrong," the creature agreed. "That's not right at all. It's gone..."

"Orange," Hiram confirmed.

"I've never seen skin do that before..."

"I'm more concerned with the fact that it feels like my flesh is melting off," Hiram shared through clenched teeth.

Phaedrus nodded and continued to stare are his arm. "I'm not a mage, Hiram. I know little spells for little things."

"Could you see if Payton is home yet?"

Phaedrus nodded. "Of course. I'll be right back." They stood and headed toward the door but first doubled back to tuck Hiram under the covers, muttering, "Just in case," to themself.

As much as his arm hurt, Hiram still managed to find it sweet.

The creature returned, not with Payton but with Mason, who looked at Hiram and asked, "Do you want me to get someone? There are other magic workers in the area. I can run to get someone. In Seneca Village, I know that there's a woman…" His eyes were fixed on Hiram's arm.

Hiram nodded, not in the mood for words.

Mason bobbed his head and left.

Phaedrus came to sit beside him, reaching out hesitantly to touch his hair, then pulling back. "We'll be all right, Hiram. I know you'll be all right."

Hiram grunted, his teeth gritted.

"It must be your hand," they said softly, eyes fixed on his arm. "It has to be. We didn't find it."

Hiram agreed but didn't voice it. Instead, he reached out with his remaining hand and gripped Phaedrus' sleeve.

The creature moved closer to him and took him into their lap, keeping him bundled in the blankets. "Hiram, you're cold," they said softly.

He nodded, pressing close to the creature; he felt frozen all over, except for his arm, which felt aflame.

They held him tighter. "Have you ever heard of the Golem of Prague? I don't imagine you have, but I'll tell it to you if you want to hear it."

Hiram nodded but didn't fully listen as the creature told him of the Maharal's golem, Josef called Yossele.

Mason returned towards the end of the second version of the story, the one where the golem fell in love. He came with a brown-skinned woman who wore a kerchief on her head and had a stern countenance.

She appraised the two of them and asked, "How long has this been?"

Phaedrus looked around the room for a clock. "About half an hour, I think. Maybe forty-five minutes."

It had felt much longer than maybe forty-five minutes.

"Can I look at him?" the woman asked, sounding kinder than she looked.

Hiram nodded and sat up, still clinging to the blankets as

best he could. She took his face into her hands, and he felt as though she'd clamped hot bricks on him.

"My name's Alma," she said. "Can you stand up?"

He nodded again and stood.

"What's troubling you?" she asked, still looking into his face, peering into his eyes and ears, checking his mouth.

He extracted his arm from the blanket, almost lost his grip on all of them in the process, and showed his arm to her. "And it hurts," he said.

She examined at his arm, her fingers cold on the parts of his skin that had gone orange. She studied the wound. "This is recent?"

He nodded.

She said, "It looks healed."

"It is," he said.

"He had an infection, but it's better now," Phaedrus offered.

Alma looked at them and nodded, more out of courtesy than acknowledgment. "Now, let's see…"

"The hand is missing," the creature said.

"I can tell," she said.

"No, I mean…we never recovered it, I don't know what became of it," Phaedrus clarified. "And…well, he left it in a mage's house. A mage who isn't happy with us."

"That is important, then, isn't it?" She inspected the stump for a while longer. "But why *orange?*" she asked. "It can't be an accident, not if it's rune magic. They don't have side effects like this. He doesn't dabble in other arts, does he?"

"Not to my knowledge," Hiram said.

"Hm," she said and peered for a little longer. She looked at Mason and asked, "Your mistress is a mage?"

He nodded.

"Is she well stocked?"

"Yes, Ms. Alma," Mason said.

"All right, you show me her stocks. I'll get this tidied," she said and to Hiram explained, "I can't get it fixed, not if he's got a piece of you, but I'll get it managed. Won't kill you at any rate. At least, I don't think so."

Hiram nodded and watched her go.

Phaedrus stood and took hold of the blankets, wrapping them more tightly around him. They put their hands on his cheeks and kissed his forehead. "See, she'll get it tidied."

"I hope so," Hiram said.

"If she can't, I'll find a way," they said. "I promised I wouldn't let you die. Come back and sit with me while you wait." They took Hiram into their arms and lifted him onto the bed, cradling him in their lap. "Now, like I was saying about the golem...you don't mind if I finish? I hate leaving a story unfinished."

"Go ahead," he said.

Phaedrus finished the story, then continued to hold Hiram, checking his forehead and telling him he was cold every few minutes.

Hiram squeezed his eyes shut and pressed his head against their chest, praying that this would end soon.

Alma returned with a bowl and a paintbrush. "Stand up, dear, and undress, if you don't mind."

He stood and shed the blankets.

Mason raised his eyebrows to see that he was already undressed.

Phaedrus cleared their throat.

Alma said nothing, but she stepped forward and dabbed the brush into the bowl. She ran the bristles over his skin and he flinched, crying out. It felt as though she had dribbled boiling oil over him.

"Shh," she soothed. "Stay still or you'll mess the lines."

Phaedrus reached out to hold his hand.

He squeezed hard as he could while Alma painted dozens of delicate designs over his chest, his arms, and legs, his back and neck, spirals and waves. The process took about ten minutes and when Alma set the brush aside, Phaedrus took their hand back, rubbing and stretching it.

Ian poked his head through the door and hesitated, staring at Hiram. "Um..."

"There's something wrong with his hand. Stump. Arm," Phaedrus said.

Ian took his eyes away from Hiram. "Should I get Payton?" he asked.

"No," Hiram said. "Not now."

The other man nodded.

Alma studied Hiram for a moment, then used her pinky to smooth the lines she had painted. Finally, she dipped her hand in the bowl and placed her hand on top of his head, sending chills down his spine. He began to sweat, and she began to chant. He trembled, and she placed her other hand on his shoulder, pushing him down so that he knelt.

As she chanted, searing heat raced through him until finally, the warmth broke in an icy rush that left him feeling faint and numb. Alma peered down at him and said, "Should be all set for a while, now. Give you time to find your missing hand."

He nodded. "Thank you."

She patted his cheek and turned to leave, saying to Mason, "Now, you'll be good and drive me home, won't you?"

"Of course, Ms. Alma," the young man said and followed her as she walked out.

Ian stared for a bit. "I'll, uh, I'll leave you, then." He edged out of the room.

Phaedrus wrapped Hiram in a blanket, scooped him up, carried him to the bathroom, and set him on the floor. They began to draw water for a bath and asked, "Didn't we just do this?"

"I believe so," he said.

"And she got it in your hair," the demon fussed. "Do you feel better?"

"It doesn't hurt as much. It's...itchy. Tingling. But it's not bad like it was before."

Phaedrus came over and touched his forehead. "Still sort of chilled. Maybe the bath will fix that."

He nodded.

"And then I'll put you back to bed. No arguing."

"I wasn't going to argue."

Phaedrus took him by the hand and helped him to stand. They walked him over to the bath and helped him climb in.

He wobbled dangerously when he lifted his leg.

Phaedrus steadied him and tutted, "This is not what I had in mind for our late morning and early afternoon together."

"I'm sorry."

"No, nothing to apologize for, Hiram. You know that," Phaedrus said.

"It wasn't that I didn't want you to..." Hiram's thoughts rushed back to when he'd had the demon behind him while he lay on his belly.

"But it is scary," Phaedrus agreed, smiling at him. "We forget, we old things, that the acts we have done so many times are still new for others."

The creature ran their hand along the surface of the water. "I wonder what that stuff is," they said, reaching out to touch the lines on his body.

"Can I have the soap?"

Phaedrus handed him the soap and a washcloth, watching contently while Hiram scrubbed himself. "You made me worry, you know. I didn't care for it."

"I'm sorry."

"I'm becoming much too fond of you," the demon informed him. "That has me worried too, but in a different way."

Hiram frowned. "Oh."

"In a good way."

The mage smiled. He did not know a good way to be worried, but he liked the way Phaedrus looked at him.

After he had bathed, Phaedrus tucked him into bed. They pulled the covers up to his chin and sat beside him. "Would you like to hear another story?" they asked.

"Yes."

"It is said that once, in the east, there was a young fisherman who, as fishermen do, lived by the sea," they began.

Hiram turned on his side and nestled into his pillow; he

closed his eyes, and Phaedrus ran their fingers through his hair.

"One day as he was walking down the beach to his boat, he came across a group of children tormenting a small sea turtle," Phaedrus continued.

Hiram listened as they continued, lulled half to sleep by their voice and their fingers in his curls.

In the following days, Hiram spent a lot of time in bed or sitting in the armchair Mason had brought up for him. Payton came and checked him over for several days, then finally declared that Alma's work had functioned just as well as any arcane magic would have.

"I thought so as well," Hiram said, propped up in bed. "Though if we had what he was using to cast it or saw his spell work that would be another case entirely."

"Still." Payton reached over to put her hand to his forehead, then touched the skin that had been turned orange. He remained cool to the touch, except for where he was orange. "Not the most flattering color. Do you feel weak, or is that just Phaedrus fussing?"

"I'm allowed to fuss," Phaedrus muttered.

"I don't feel wonderful, to be honest," he said, "but I don't know that I need constant minding."

Phaedrus crossed their arms.

"Which I appreciate, of course, Phaedrus." He gave the creature a warm smile.

They smiled back and placed their hand on his head.

"Hopefully, this enemy of yours will surface soon," Payton

said. "I'd like to get all this dealt with."

Ian, who had been standing back and to the side, nodded.

"And maybe then I will have my husband back," she said with a glance at Ian.

Hiram frowned. "What do you mean?"

"He's been eavesdropping outside your door," she said.

Ian blushed. "No, I..."

"He likes your stories, Phaedrus," Payton said.

Ian turned even redder.

"I like him a lot better like this," the demon said. Ian had, around his guests, dropped his air of debauched wealth and sex. "You can come into the room and listen."

"I didn't wish to intrude," the young man said.

"No, you're very welcome to join us," Hiram assured.

Payton touched his forehead one last time and said, "I'm going uptown to see my parents. I don't expect you're feeling up to the trip?"

Hiram shook his head. Payton's parents terrified him, and he didn't want to imagine what they would do if they set eyes on Phaedrus. Their daughter may have been sexually adventurous and lacked some scruples, but the elder Mr. and Mrs. Reinhart collected rare things and rare people and kept them in their home, passed off as servants. The ones that tried to get away ended up as decorations; a pink lampshade made of fairy skin or a carpet fringed with dark brown werewolf fur or, hidden from most guests, the pretty eyes of a mouthy servant kept in a jar.

They had visited Fall's Hill in his youth, each time bringing some exotic creature or foreigner with them, and several times they had returned North with a slave they had thought particularly striking. An albino born of African parents or a dark-skinned boy with blue eyes, a pale brown girl with freckles and red curls. Hiram remained sure that they had visited and sent Payton to visit in an attempt to find the books that were now missing. A few dozen demons would have made nice showpieces.

"I didn't think so," she said. "We'll be very careful not to mention that your books are missing, won't we, Ian?"

Ian nodded, clearly not sure why that would be of interest to his in-laws. "Of course not."

"We'll be home in a few hours. Let Mason know if you need anything," she said and then left, putting her hand on her husband's arm as they walked out together.

"It seems nice, what they have," Phaedrus said.

Hiram glanced at them. "Money? Lunatic parents?"

"No," Phaedrus said. "The three of them seem happy together. Payton and Ian, Ian and Mason. It's working out nicely."

"Oh. Yes," Hiram agreed.

Ian and Mason, when they believed that people weren't paying attention, would share tender looks and sweet words. Payton smiled when she noticed, biting her lip in an attempt to hide the happiness she had for her husband. Knowing what he did of her, Hiram assumed she didn't want to seem syrupy; Reinharts were not, as a rule, syrupy or sentimental, and very rarely romantic.

"Her parents would skin him alive if they knew," Hiram added after a few moments of thought.

"Ian?"

"No. Mason. Ian, they would just make miserable for the rest of his life," he said.

"Miserable family, really," Phaedrus said.

Hiram hesitated for a minute and admitted, "It's horrible, but I'm glad my father is dead."

The demon looked at him.

"It's...he was my father, of course, we were family...but the things he did."

"I understand a thing or two about having problems with your father," they said.

Hiram glanced up, then felt stupid. "Right, of course."

The demon reached over to touch his curls.

Hiram stood and stretched, though doing so left him light-headed. He swayed.

Phaedrus reached out to steady him.

"Thank you, but I'm—"

"You are not fine, Hiram. You've been cursed or hexed or something like it." They brought him close to their chest and rested their chin on his head.

"And we're working on fixing it," Hiram replied. He looked up and kissed the creature on their lips. "Worrier."

"Why did you get up, anyway? You should be resting."

Hiram snorted and went over to the desk against the wall. He spent a minute or so making sure that everything he would need was in reach of his remaining hand so he would not need to get up again, then sat, taking up a pen and setting it to paper.

"Who are you writing to?"

"I received a letter from Ellen this morning," he said. "I'm writing back." Hiram handed the demon the letter, marked with penmanship that was neat but unmistakably belonged to a beginner.

Phaedrus skimmed it then returned it, saying, "She seems bright."

Hiram nodded. He wrote for several minutes, letting her know that he was well and that they would be able to come home soon. With Blackwell still unaccounted for, he wanted them somewhere safe, and there was no one he trusted better than Susan to keep his family safe.

"The story about the fisherman's wife," he said when he had finished the letter.

"What about it?"

"It's not your favorite story."

Phaedrus said, "No, of course not. I wasn't going to tell my favorite story to a stranger. But it is a *good* story. I like it."

"I'm not a stranger now, though."

"No."

"So what's your favorite story?"

Phaedrus regarded him for a moment, then said, "Come back to bed, and we'll make ourselves cozy."

Although the demon's insistence on bedrest chafed at him, the offer to cuddle close to them was something he didn't think he would ever refuse. "If I rest all day today, tomorrow will you let me go for a walk?"

"I let you go for a walk today."

"Around the house," Hiram said, "For five minutes."

"Tomorrow, if I feel you're up to it, we will go for a walk."

"Generous of you."

The demon met him at the bed, turning the covers back, and they settled themselves in. "Comfortable?" Phaedrus asked.

With their arms around him and his head on their chest, Hiram could not think of a better place to be. "Yes."

"It's a very long story, though, Hiram," they warned. "You must promise you won't ask me to start it without letting me finish."

"I'll hear the whole thing, as long as it takes."

Kissing his forehead, they said, "I hope you mean that. It is told that once, in ancient times, there was a king who ruled over the countries of India and China. He was a king of great wealth, with many possessions, many troops, and servants to see that his will was done. He had two sons, the elder called Shahriyár and the younger called Sháh-Zemán..."

Hiram said, "This does sound like a long story."

"Shh."

"Am I not allowed to interrupt?"

"Not to say silly things like that. Real questions and comments only, please," they said.

"Oh, yes..." Hiram began but trailed off. He had meant to give a falsely subservient answer, a 'yes sir' or a 'yes ma'am', but he did not know which title he could apply to the creature.

The creature glanced at him. "You could call me Your Majesty. I'm rather fond of that."

Hiram smiled and asked, "Are you going to finish telling the story?"

"There came a time when the elder one wished to see his brother," they continued, taking Hiram's hand and resting it on their chest, rubbing their thumb on the back of his hand.

They continued the tale until Mason knocked lightly on the door and Hiram called for him to come in.

"We've prepared something to eat if you're hungry," he said.

"Thank you very much, Mason. We'll be down shortly," Phaedrus said.

After they ate and Ian and Payton had returned home, Phaedrus resumed their story, and Hiram became very sure the demon's tale would not end for a very long time. They spent the evening together, all four of them, in the parlor with beverages in hand and a fire in the grate while Phaedrus continued their tale.

Mason refreshed their drinks several times until Payton grabbed him by the sleeve and said, "Sit."

He sat on the sofa between her and Ian, stiff and straight.

She placed her drink in his hand and informed him, "You shouldn't fuss over us so much, it makes you seem overeager."

"Sorry, ma'am," he said.

"When you seem overeager, people begin to wonder why," she said, and it sounded to Hiram like she was giving the young man a warning. "You don't want anyone wondering about you."

"No," he said.

Hiram sat up from the chair he had slumped in, half-nodding off while he listened to the creature's story. "Payton," he said.

"Nothing to worry about, Hiram," she said.

"You can tell me," he said. He had once, in their childhoods, been privy to many of her secrets.

"I expect that my parents will be visiting more often. It is best that some things remain unknown to them," she said.

He nodded. "Why?"

"Because they are lunatics, Hiram," she said.

"No, why will they be visiting?" he asked.

"Oh. Right. Because of the baby."

Hiram blinked and thought for a moment; it took a little

while for the pieces to slide into place because Payton was the exact opposite of what he thought of when he thought of a mother. She had no soft spot for children or small animals; she had never expressed any desire to have a child, not even in the vaguest way. "Congratulations, both of you," he offered uncertainly.

"Thank you," she said, just as uncertainly.

He looked at Ian, who appeared more excited.

He had taken the other young man's hand in his. "It is something I've always hoped for," Ian said.

Hiram nodded.

Phaedrus said, "You'll do well, as long as you don't teach the babe to put on the same airs that you do."

Ian turned pink around the ears.

"And if you don't let your parents get their hooks in," Hiram suggested mildly into his drink.

Payton glanced at him, then announced to the room, "I think I'll retire for the night. No, Ian, you stay. I want a little time to myself."

He nodded and squeezed her hand before she left.

Shortly after Payton left, Hiram and Phaedrus went to bed, leaving Ian and Mason alone on the couch.

"Do you wonder which one is the father?" Phaedrus asked quietly.

Hiram glanced at them; the thought had not occurred to him. "No."

"I mean...they don't look alike. If it comes out looking...unlike either of its parents..." the demon said. "They're both blond, and Mason is not."

"Both of her parents have dark hair," Hiram said. "I'm not even sure that Payton and Mason *are* sleeping together, I think it might just be him and Ian. I don't know. It isn't any of my business anyway."

"Of course," Phaedrus said.

After they had been in bed for an hour, Phaedrus nudged him. "I sort of get the feeling that they have, though, her and Mason. Don't you get that feeling? Even a little?"

"Please go to sleep," Hiram said.

"It's only a thought."

Hiram took a pillow and put it over the creature's face. "Go to sleep."

Phaedrus took the pillow from their face and then nestled close to Hiram.

TWO MORE days passed with Hiram still fatigued and now slightly shaky. It concerned him somewhat, though he did his best to hide it from the others. He was in no mood to be fussed over anymore, especially when there was nothing that could be done to help, not without Blackwell.

Phaedrus had, after much insistence and assurance that Hiram would be fine, gone out with Payton and Mason to pick up some dresses from the tailor. Payton had insisted that she needed companionship and that Phaedrus needed to leave the house.

"Are you still alive?" Ian peeked his head into the room without knocking.

"Still," Hiram confirmed.

"I'd hoped so. She...they," he corrected himself, "would be devastated otherwise."

Hiram nodded, not knowing what to add. Agreement, he felt, would be haughty.

"Anyway, a message came from Lysander's."

Hiram sat up straighter, pushing the covers aside and swinging his legs out of bed. "What does it say?"

Ian held out the note to him. "I didn't open it."

Hiram took it and skimmed it, then read it more slowly. "Blackwell's made contact."

The younger man blinked. "Oh. Well...uh. Now what?"

"Lysander's has arranged to meet with him this evening at seven," Hiram said, then reread the note to make sure he'd understood it totally.

"We'll have to go, then. When the other two return."

Hiram nodded.

Ian put a hand on his shoulder. "You don't have to be so worried. We'll get this handled and you back home safe."

Hiram had not thought his nervousness would be so apparent. "I'm sure everything will be fine."

Ian smiled at him, a kind smile that nevertheless didn't make Hiram feel any better. He appeared just as worried as Hiram felt. He and Hiram looked at each other until finally, Ian said, "I've never been brave."

"There's no such thing as brave," Hiram said. "At least, I've never felt brave..."

Ian nodded. "I know what you mean." He hesitated then asked, "Do you want to eat something?"

Hiram nodded.

By the time they'd finished eating, Payton and Phaedrus had returned with Mason carrying several boxes. Hiram shared the note with them, and they both immediately began to speak at the same time. He made no effort to listen to what they said until they had calmed down.

"We have to get there early," Phaedrus said, the first thing that came through clearly, not jumbled with Payton's voice.

"Of course."

"You shouldn't come," they added, their arms crossed.

"Don't be ridiculous."

"Hiram, you're a mess."

"I'm well enough for this."

"Lives are at risk, including both of ours. We cannot afford to make an error," they said, firm but not unkind.

"I won't make an error," Hiram said. "I've made it this far. I'm not going to sit out and send you off against him."

Phaedrus adjusted their arms and said, "I—"

"Let's not argue," Payton said. "Please. We need a plan, not a lover's quarrel."

The demon let out a breath through their nose, and Hiram nodded. Payton came to sit at the table, and Phaedrus took a seat as well.

Folding her hands on the table, Payton said, "Tell me what you know of this mage. For what kind of magic do I need to prepare?"

Hiram said, "He's a mage of some talent but not practiced, to my knowledge, in anything other than rune magic." He glanced at Phaedrus, who shrugged.

"I've never seen him do anything else," the creature agreed.

"Good," Payton said. "Considering that he's stooped to stealing resources, I don't think I'll have much trouble with him. What is talent in the small cities of Canada is not much compared to our family."

Ian glanced between his wife and her cousin and said, hesitantly, "He gave Hiram trouble, though."

With a smile that worried Hiram, Payton said, "Hiram is much nicer than I am."

With his eyebrows furrowed, Ian said, "Oh."

Payton reached over to pat his hand. "Don't worry, you won't ever see that side of me."

He nodded.

She squeezed his hand and stood. "I need to change into something more suitable and prepare a few things. A half-hour and then we'll head over?"

Hiram and Phaedrus nodded.

She left.

Hiram and Phaedrus returned to their room. Phaedrus said nothing and went to sit on the bed, looking down at their hand, examining their nails and cuticles.

"What is it?" Hiram asked.

"Those other things Blackwell was looking for...the basilisk feathers or whatever they were. You knew the spell for which they're needed."

Hiram nodded.

"What spell?"

"For binding," Hiram said. "For binding what you are. Indefinitely."

"I'd worried as much. It would be worse than dying."

"If you were to die, I wouldn't be able to save you," Hiram said. "But I would do everything to free you."

"I don't like either scenario," they said. "And this dictionary...we've dangled the last thing he needs in front of him. He may be very determined to get it."

"Phaedrus."

"I know. I'm worrying. But I've started a story, and it would be terrible not to finish it..." they said, still looking at their hands.

Hiram sat beside them.

"And this is something good, Hiram, between us, something I haven't had in years, and I would see this through as well."

Hiram wished June had given him the exact date on his gravestone so that he would know if that day had passed yet. He felt sure it must have, but there was nothing stopping it from changing again. When he had been a youth, twenty-six had seemed so far away and old, bordering on elderly, but now that he had those twenty-six years behind him, they seemed short and insufficient to prepare him for the rest of his life.

"You'll live forever, won't you?" he asked.

The demon looked up. "Unless something stops me. Why?"

Hiram shook his head.

"I don't have any sort of prejudice against old age if that's what you're worried about," Phaedrus said. "Twenty or forty or eighty, it's all the same to me."

"The undying keep their love from mortals."

"We certainly try, but you're everywhere," Phaedrus said.

"Phaedrus, I am mortal."

"I know."

"Does that happen a lot, that someone dies and you go on?"

"A few times," they admitted. "It's...worth it, though. To know that a person was cared for and loved for all their years, to make someone happy and live a life together."

"You don't wish you'd been with another person like you? Another who wouldn't die?"

"Just because someone won't die doesn't mean they won't leave you," Phaedrus said.

"Oh."

"Not to mention, I've met humans who have become undying. Vampires. Almost always a tragedy, if you ask me, and the rest...well, your whole family dies, your lover casts you aside and you're abandoned in a world totally different from the one you knew. And...you know, even among those who are naturally long-lived, there is the issue of madness. My king's children are sadly prone to such things."

"I wasn't implying—"

"I'm not saying you were. Just what I've noticed. I meant it when I said I don't care about age. My feelings are for you."

Hiram leaned against them. "We should go soon."

"I think you should stay."

"And I think I shouldn't," he said.

Phaedrus looked at him for a moment then touched his face. They leaned over and kissed him deeply. When they pulled back, they said, "As soon as you are well again, Hiram, the things I want to do to you."

Hiram licked his lips. "We could do them now."

"You're all cold and shaky. I'll wait," the demon said. "I'd be horrified if you passed out."

Hiram blushed. "I didn't think you'd noticed the shaking."

The demon kissed him on the temple. "I notice a lot of things. Shall we go?"

"Yes."

Phaedrus stood and rummaged through their suitcase for

a moment, finally taking out a knife and hiding it on their person. Then they took Hiram by the hand and met up with Payton in the foyer.

Ian stood slightly behind her, his fingers twisted in Mason's.

Hiram glanced at them and then at his cousin.

"He's not a mage, and he's not a fighter. I'd rather have him safe," Payton said, "And too many people will make this more difficult."

"See, and *he* listens," Phaedrus murmured to Hiram, a half-smile on his lips.

Hiram rolled his eyes.

Payton said, "Mason, have that room prepared for when we return. It needs to be just so."

"Yes, ma'am," Mason said.

Payton gestured for her guests to follow, and together they entered the carriage that waited to bring them to Lysander's.

THEY WAITED, crowded close in a small room off to the side of Lysander's office. The room, in truth, was not much more than a closet. Phaedrus had positioned themself behind Hiram, their arm around his waist and their chin resting on his shoulder. It was odd for Hiram to have someone around who matched his height, but it was also refreshing, no longer leaving him to feel like an awkward giant.

His heart was in his throat, and his body buzzed with nerves; having Phaedrus hold him quelled the feeling somewhat, but their touch was a blanket in the face of a snowstorm.

Lysander had been nervous too, and they could all hear it in his voice as he greeted Blackwell. They had all agreed to give the man a little while to settle in and for the woman who kept his books to bar the door to keep him from escaping should something go wrong.

As soon as he heard the other mage's voice, Hiram's heartbeat doubled, and he felt ill.

Phaedrus tightened their grip and nuzzled their face against his neck. "He won't hurt you again," they promised.

Hiram bit his lip and nodded, on the verge of tears and

hoping that the demon had not been right about him staying behind.

From the wall to their backs, they heard two knocks. All had gone well: the right man had come and come alone; the door had been barred. Payton placed her hand on Hiram's shoulder, and by the light from Phaedrus' eyes, he saw her nod. He took a breath, the demon released him, and Payton reached for the doorknob.

The two of them burst through the door with Phaedrus hanging back a little. As they chanted their spells, Blackwell stared for a moment, then cried, "You!"

He began to call a spell back, but their work rendered him unconscious before he finished. He slumped in his chair and the mages worked magical bindings over, quickly but methodically.

Hiram stared down at him when they had finished, his body trembling. Payton took back her dictionary and gave Lysander a significant amount of money; she then rapped on the door once then twice, and they heard the barrier behind slide away.

None of them spoke, worried that something would go wrong between this too-easy kidnapping and home.

Once the door was opened, Phaedrus lifted Blackwell's unconscious body and walked out, heading for the carriage that awaited them. They dumped the man unceremoniously on the floor and climbed inside. The Reinharts followed suit, and they all sat tersely on the drive back.

When they arrived home, Phaedrus brought him inside and looked at Mason, who gestured for them to follow. The young man took them to a room that had been stripped bare of everything but a few pieces of furniture. A chair sat in the middle of the room with a dark, rough sheet beneath it.

Hiram hesitated at the doorway of the room, though Payton did not. She entered right behind Phaedrus and said, "In the chair. Tie him tightly."

The demon obeyed then stepped back.

Payton glanced at Blackwell. "Hiram, are you coming in?"

He entered and closed the door behind him.

She studied their captive for a moment. "What is your priority?" she asked.

"The hand," Phaedrus answered, though Hiram had intended to say the books. "He needs to get this hex with the hand undone."

"I'm sure they're all in the same place," Hiram said after a moment. "The hand and the books. Find where he's staying."

Payton nodded, rubbed her hands together and went over to Blackwell. She lifted a small, thin blade from the table, tilted his head back and carved a half dozen runes into his forehead.

Phaedrus stared, reaching over to take Hiram's hand while she worked. "Goodness," the demon muttered.

"It's insurance," she said, "Even if he breaks his bonds, his magic will be dormant. It is much more permanent than those cuffs."

"How permanent?" Phaedrus asked.

"He'd have to erase the runes entirely and then apply new ones to undo this spell," Hiram said, "Burning or sanding works well enough for the first part, but then it's hard to apply new runes to scarred skin."

The demon looked at him, seeming shocked that he would know the answer.

Payton set her blade down and tapped Blackwell's cheek. He didn't stir so she muttered a spell that sent a jolt through him, and he snapped to consciousness, letting out a guttural cry.

"The books and the hand," she said, "Tell me where they are."

"Release me immediately," Blackwell demanded.

"The books and the hand or I will begin to ask with serious intent," she warned.

Blackwell looked at Phaedrus, his eyes fixed on the demon. "This freak—"

Payton sent another jolt through him. "We were talking about something." She glanced at the other two. "Perhaps it would be better…less distracting if you waited elsewhere."

Phaedrus nodded and took Hiram by the arm, leading him out of the room. Almost as soon as the door closed, they heard Blackwell let out a real scream.

"She'll get an answer," Hiram said. "She's…relentless."

The demon nodded and then reached out a hand to touch Hiram, running their hand through his curls and resting it on his cheek. "This is going too well. It was too easy."

"Don't say that until we're done," he said, reaching up to touch the hand on his cheek, putting his own hand over Phaedrus' and nestling against the demon's palm.

Blackwell cried out again.

"I wish I didn't feel bad for him," Phaedrus said.

"I wonder if it will change his perspective on torturing people."

"I don't know," the demon said.

They took him by the hand and led him to the living room, where Mason and Ian already sat. Upon seeing them, Mason asked, "Is there anything I can get for you?"

"No, thank you," they said together.

The young man leaned back against Ian, who looked pale and worried.

"What's wrong?" Phaedrus asked.

"I've never…this side of her, it's unfamiliar to me," Ian admitted.

"You didn't know her when she was fourteen. She tormented the daylights out of all the men she came across," Hiram said, "She hated me for years because she couldn't get me to fall in line."

"What changed?" Ian asked.

Hiram shrugged. "I told her. About how I felt. Regarding, well, men." He glanced at Phaedrus then said, "Or, I suppose, how I don't feel about women."

They heard Blackwell scream again, and no one could look anyone else in the eyes for a moment.

"Maybe we should have tried something else first," Hiram

said softly, looking at the floor.

No one agreed with him, but no one told him they had done the right thing either. They all sat for a few more minutes until Hiram stood.

"Where are you going?" Phaedrus asked.

He shook his head and said, "I can't."

The demon did not follow him or ask anything else.

He reentered the room where Payton had Blackwell.

She looked over at him.

He approached her, putting a hand on her arm and turning her away from Blackwell's gaze. "There has to be something else," he whispered.

"I'm sure there is, Hiram, but I'll get results with this."

"It doesn't feel right."

"Well...Strictly speaking, it isn't right," she said, unbothered.

He rubbed his eyes.

She put her hand on his shoulder and said, "I'll do something about the noise. I should anyway, though the neighbors wouldn't dare to say anything."

"Payton."

"Don't worry so much," she said and gave him a gentle push towards the door.

He left and returned to the others. He sat and said nothing.

After a few minutes, Ian said, "Hiram, you have a...a, uh, a daughter, don't you?"

"No."

"Oh, I...I thought that you'd received a letter from a young girl."

"Ellen is my niece."

"Oh, I see."

Ian said nothing after that.

Phaedrus reached over and put their hand on Hiram's arm. "Come for a walk?"

"Hmm?"

"It's a nice day, very nearly lovely. Come out for a walk,"

they said, standing and tugging at his shirtsleeve.

He stood, glancing at Ian and Mason for a moment, then followed behind Phaedrus. The creature offered him their arm, and he took it, feeling a little strange for just a moment. Many things recently had disturbed the quiet equilibrium of his life, and it was bizarre that something so little as being offered an arm to go for a stroll could do so. He wondered if he found it jarring because he was, as a man, ingrained to be the one offering his arm or because Phaedrus was very much not a man. Perhaps if it had been Julian, it would not have seemed strange.

The thought went as quickly as it came, gone before they had exited the house.

Night had fallen, though just barely. The whole affair with Blackwell had not taken more than two hours. Phaedrus kept a steady grip on his arm, their jade hand warm even through his shirt, and he still felt chilled despite the warmth of the night. He missed Georgia; he missed the heat, slick and fetid, comforting in the way the smell of horses was comforting.

June had complained endlessly of the heat. Hiram assumed it must have been a love that had to be nurtured from infancy.

"Dry heat," June had said to him once. "Give me a desert but no more of this dampness."

"What are you thinking about?" Phaedrus asked.

"Junius," he answered.

"Should I be jealous?" they teased.

He shook his head. "Something he said about the heat once."

"Maybe someday you'll take me there," the demon suggested.

"I can't go back," he said.

"When you're old," they said.

Hiram glanced at them. "Where did you grow up?"

"Heaven," they said without hesitation. "I was made as soon as the others started telling stories. Someone had to keep track."

"And God couldn't?" Hiram asked, feeling blasphemous.

"Couldn't? No, of course He could. He didn't want to," Phaedrus said. "I've, obviously, since been replaced."

"Impossible," Hiram said.

The demon looked at him fondly but said nothing. They walked together for a long time, stepping around the unpleasant things that littered their path here and there. Hiram continued to dwell in his thoughts of home, of sweltering summers and skin that shone with sweat. As a younger man, he had found his eyes fixed on the men who labored in the sun, precipitation making them gleam like oiled athletes.

It had been strange, watching those beautiful, dark men, knowing he would never have them but knowing there would have been nothing they could have done to stop him. That idea had left a bad taste in his mouth, a taste that had, coupled with his brother's death, his nanny's tears and his niece's abuse, propelled him toward the never-warm-enough city he now called home.

"What's going on in that busy little mind of yours?" Phaedrus asked, pulling him back to the present.

"Greek wrestlers."

"What about them?"

"Did they really oil themselves?"

Phaedrus nodded.

Hiram found his tongue moving to wet his lips. Suddenly Phaedrus moved to cover his mouth with theirs, pulling him close. The kiss was brief, but Hiram found himself breathing hard when the demon pulled away.

Giving him hardly a moment to recover, Phaedrus continued walking, keeping their grip on his arm.

The walk they took did not last an incredibly long time, nothing compared to the hours he had spent walking Falls' Hill, but by the time they returned to Payton's home, Hiram had grown tired. Phaedrus chatted pleasantly as they readied for bed and Hiram could hardly keep his eyes open.

The creature tucked him into bed, and Hiram settled in, only to push himself up a few minutes later to say, "Check on him. Blackwell. See what Payton's done."

"I will."

Hiram lay back down. "Promise."

"Of course. Go to sleep," they said.

Hiram did.

THE LIGHT woke Hiram slowly the following morning. He dozed on and off for an hour or so until he finally opened his eyes and sat up. He spied Phaedrus wrapped in a dressing robe, sitting in an armchair with a newspaper in hand.

"Good morning."

Hiram rubbed his eyes, ran a hand through his hair and let out a sigh. He stretched and said, "Morning. What time is it?"

"Half-past eleven."

Hiram felt mildly shocked. "Oh."

Sensibly, the demon said, "You aren't well. It's to be expected."

"Wasted the day..."

"Payton is still at work. We've time to waste." They folded their newspaper and set it aside. "Have a bath. It will be time to eat by the time you're done."

Hiram rubbed his eyes, then got out of bed, not liking the way the creature frowned at him.

Phaedrus noticed him looking. "The sooner this is done the better."

Hiram couldn't argue. After he bathed and dressed, they

joined the others for a light lunch. Mason moved between the kitchen and standing behind Ian, looking nervous, and Payton said hardly a thing to anyone. When she set aside her napkin and stood, Hiram asked, "How is it?"

"I have one last thing to try," she said. "If that does not work, I'll be reduced to asking my parents for help. Let's hope it doesn't come to that."

The mage nodded.

His cousin left after that, and the four of them who remained dispersed in pairs, Ian looking drawn and Hiram feeling faint.

Phaedrus took him by the elbow and keep a hold on his arm.

"I must look much worse than I feel," Hiram tried to joke, but the creature did not laugh.

While they waited to hear from Payton, Hiram reread the last letter he had gotten from Ellen.

Phaedrus watched him, arms crossed and mouth turned down.

Hiram did not ask what bothered them.

As the sun started to hang low in the sky, someone knocked on their door.

"Come in," they called at the same time.

Mason entered and said, "She's done it."

Phaedrus moved towards the door and Hiram followed behind; they encountered Payton in the foyer. She had a calmness over her that unsettled Hiram and made him want to ask what she had done to finally get a result. He would not really want to hear the answer, so he remained quiet.

"Not going without me, are you?" Phaedrus asked.

"I knew you would be along," she said.

The demon looked at Hiram and said, without much conviction, "I want you to stay here."

"No."

The creature sighed but didn't protest again. Their carriage ride to Blackwell's residence was quiet, interrupted only by sounds from the street. They arrived at a high-end boarding house, and the other two followed behind Payton as she entered. She did not stop at the desk, but headed up the stairs, taking a key from her pocket as she walked.

When he looked more closely, he saw blood beneath her nails and looked away.

She unlocked the door, pushed it open and then waited for a moment in the doorway. They all glanced at each other.

Phaedrus took Hiram by the hand before they headed inside.

Payton called up several lights and they split off to search the room.

"He wasn't specific about *where* everything was, but it's not a big room," she said.

Hiram pulled his hand back from Phaedrus' so they could search more efficiently. He looked through the desk and found a skeletal hand with the bones held together by silver wires. With a degree of hesitation, he took the hand from the drawer, feeling that it must be his. He peered at the bones and saw that they had been carefully penned all over with runes.

As he peered at them, he began to giggle.

The other two looked at him.

"What?" Phaedrus asked.

He held up his skeletal hand.

"Ugh!" They wrinkled their nose.

"The runes, though," he said and giggled again. "The rune he used is *tal*, and he must have meant...I mean, when you read it, he must have meant *tol*, which is melting. He got the third serif off the ascender wrong."

"And what's *tal*?" Phaedrus asked.

"Orange," Payton said.

"Can you undo it?"

Hiram eyed the bones for a little longer, then glanced around the desk. He opened several vials, sniffing them until he found a solvent. He ripped a scrap off a shirt he found and used it to rub out the ink on the bones, chanting over them to nullify what remained of the spell. He didn't feel immediately better, but he felt no worse and considered that a good thing.

He held the bones in his hand for a moment, not sure what to do with them until Payton offered, "Would you like me to put that in my bag?"

He nodded and handed them over.

"It will be interesting to keep on your mantle," she said with a small smile. She turned away and went back to the suitcase she'd been searching.

Hiram glanced around the room and spied a trunk sticking out from under the bed. He knelt and pulled it out. He tugged at the buckle and undid it without incident. When he flipped the lid open, he heard a small pop followed by a sound like a blade being taken from its sheath. He felt something hit his chest but paid it no mind.

"I found the books," he said, or attempted to say, but his words came out garbled.

Phaedrus turned to look at him, frowning, and then their eyes went wide and they knelt beside him, their hands unsure. "Hiram," they whispered.

Hiram reached up to touch his chest and found a ragged, gaping wound gushing blood down his shirt. The sight of his blood, of the wound, made him feel suddenly lightheaded, full of panic and adrenaline. "Phaedrus..."

"No," the demon whispered, reaching out to touch his face. The protest was quiet, the closest to meek the creature had ever sounded, and Hiram worried. Tears slipped from their silver eyes, down their cheeks, and they said, "No, it can't end like this."

Phaedrus pulled Hiram into their arms, their embrace careful but firm. The creature whispered to themself.

Praying, Hiram realized, the thought dull and far away. He felt cold, much colder than he had with his hand cursed. It became clear to him that this was his end, that whatever death he had avoided with June's warning had only been delayed.

He didn't panic or balk. He felt cold and tired, and couldn't think much beyond a sort of vague wonder that *this* was all his life had been.

Phaedrus began to speak, in a low desperate voice, no

longer praying but demanding something. "You have to fix it. I can't lose him."

"Why should I?" asked a voice that Hiram did not know. The voice did not seem to be making a serious inquiry, but to almost be teasing.

"There isn't *time* for this," Phaedrus growled.

Something knelt beside Hiram, taking him by the shoulders and cradling him against the chest. "Give me room," a voice said.

Phaedrus retreated.

Hiram clutched their sleeve.

"I'm right here," Phaedrus promised, their hands wrapped around his. "You'll be well soon."

That didn't make sense. He turned his eyes to the stranger and found an almost-human face with milk-pale skin and terrible eyes.

With spidery long hands, the newcomer opened Hiram's mouth and dribbled something in, something harsh and foul from a small red bottle.

Hiram gagged on it.

The stranger smiled down at him and tipped back Hiram's chin so he couldn't cough anything up.

Hiram felt that this thing would devour him.

Instead, it pressed one hand to the wound on his chest and Hiram began to feel excruciatingly hot, breaking into a sweat.

A moment later the creature released him, then stood. It wiped its fingers, dark with Hiram's blood, on to Phaedrus' shirt. "All taken care of," it said, "Now you and he will have a nice, long eternity together."

Phaedrus paled. "What?"

Hiram tried to sit him.

Phaedrus put a hand on a shoulder to keep him still. "What did you do?" they demanded softly.

From the floor, Hiram got a better view of their visitor. A man, perhaps, spindly and taller than anyone Hiram had ever seen.

"Threw it in for free," the man said, grinning awfully. "A gift from your favorite big brother."

"I didn't ask for that!"

"Ah, well..." the man said. He glanced down at Hiram on the floor. His face faltered a little. Hiram didn't know what to make of the blend of guilt, concern, and boredom. The expression disappeared when he turned back to Phaedrus.

"Undo it," Phaedrus demanded. They climbed to their feet, drawn to their full height but still not as tall as the stranger.

"I can't," the man said placidly.

Phaedrus grabbed the man by his shirt, pulling him close so the little red bottle dropped from his fingers. "You did it, you can undo it!"

"No," he said calmly. "Unless you want me to kill him altogether. I can bestow, but it is uncommonly difficult to...un-bestow." He put his hand on Phaedrus' and removed their hand from his shirt. "Besides, he's a Reinhart. I have plans for them anyway. Long run stuff. You wouldn't be interested."

"I am incredibly interested in his long run," Phaedrus said.

Hiram sat up.

"Oh, you should rest, though, little one," the man said. "It was still a mighty wound."

Being directly addressed by the newcomer, whatever he was, made Hiram's skin crawl. A deep unease burrowed into him, deeper the longer the man kept his eyes on Hiram's.

Phaedrus came over and helped Hiram up, keeping their arm tight around him. "Hiram, I'm sorry."

The man said, in a kinder tone, "Don't worry too much, Phaedrus. There's a happy ending in this for you if you two can wait it out. You know...I have these plans..." He gave a vague wave of his hands.

Phaedrus shook their head. "You aren't the man you were."

"I'm not the woman I used to be either," he said,

grinning so wide his face might split. "Things will be well." He patted Phaedrus on the face. "I promise."

Phaedrus looked unsure, but their anger seemed to have abated. "You assume so much," they said, disappointed.

The man shrugged. "Not my worst trait. See you soon." With that, the man disappeared as unobtrusively as he'd arrived.

Hiram looked at Phaedrus, touched the place where there had been a hole in his chest, and said, "Who was that?"

"My king."

Hiram felt a small wave of blank shock move over him. "Bad blood between you two?"

"No...but we worry for him, all of us. The place where he reigns is a place made of nightmares, and it does little for his mind," Phaedrus said. "He does things that he would not have done before. He should *not* have done that."

Hiram nodded. "But you asked him to."

"No, I asked him to save your life not..." Phaedrus sighed. They cradled Hiram's face in their hand. "But he saved your life." They pressed their lips together.

"That's not so bad," Hiram noted weakly.

"No."

Payton came over and took the books from the trunk, slipping them into her bag. She calmly pointed out, "Not that I'm not horrified by what just happened, but we should go before anything else tries to kill one of us."

Phaedrus nodded, keeping their arm around Hiram the entire way home.

PAYTON RETURNED his books once they arrived back at her house, and he brought them up to his room, placing them on top of his suitcase. He felt Phaedrus watching him and knew they had something serious to discuss. It would be easier to ignore what had happened, the suspicions he had. Finally, he turned and asked, "What did he do to me?"

"The last thing I wanted for you."

"In simple terms, Phaedrus," he said.

"He's prolonged your life, your youth, perhaps made it eternal."

Hiram nodded, touching his chest again.

"If I had known..."

"Better than being dead, though, isn't it?" Hiram asked with a small smile.

"You will linger long past all that you care for. The world will change, in horrible ways sometimes."

The mage looked down at his shoes. "You wanted me to get old, didn't you?"

"I wanted to give you a beautiful life, Hiram. A complete one. Not a stretched-out, unnatural one that will end in tragedy."

"Sounds like a promise," Hiram said. "Perhaps it can be undone. I can write to the university."

He sighed and went to sit on the side of the bed closest to him, facing away from the creature, not sure why such a heavy feeling had grown in his gut, spreading up to his chest and throat. He looked down, at his hand and at his stump. He had made a lot of assumptions about what would happen when this was over. He'd come up with silly ideas that now seemed impractical, even stupid, especially faced with the demon's disappointment in his new status.

Phaedrus came to sit beside him, putting an arm around his shoulders. It felt like an embrace that would be followed by bad news. It was, Hiram remembered, exactly what Susan had done when she'd come to tell him to say goodbye to his mother.

"Does it change things?" he asked.

"I don't know."

A very unreasonable thought came over him, one that made tears well up in his eyes.

"Hiram!" the demon said, their voice full of quiet shock. "What's wrong?"

"You wanted me to die," Hiram said.

"No!" they protested, "Not...Hiram, not like that! Mercy, what a horribly grim thing to think."

Uncomforted, Hiram began to weep.

The demon put both arms around him and held him close. "What did *you* mean by changing things?"

"The way you feel about me."

"Oh, Hiram, *no*," they said. "I just meant...I don't know, about...*how* we're going to live a life together."

Hiram nestled further into Phaedrus' arms, still feeling insecure.

The demon rubbed his back. "I'm still very fond of you, even if things aren't quite the way they were. I'd like to continue as we'd discussed, this...change aside."

Hiram sniffled.

"Does that satisfy you?"

"No."

"Hiram, if I had wanted you to die, I would have left you to die on that floor. A mortal man is meant to have a mortal life. Some day you'll understand what exactly it is I'm mourning."

Feeling rather like a child, Hiram asked, "But you still care for me?"

"Of course. And we got the books and that nonsense with your hand resolved. Nothing to cry about."

Hiram hugged them close.

"I mean...you did almost die, so you can certainly cry if you'd like," they said. They leaned in close and kissed his curls. "Although...you should get out of these clothes."

Hiram pulled back and looked down at himself. He nodded in agreement, wiping his eyes on his sleeve. He tossed his clothes into a pile in the bathroom and eyed the pink scar that had the wound had left.

Phaedrus clucked their tongue. "Sloppy work on his part."

They drew a bath for him, taking something out of their own suitcase and drizzling it into the water. They tested the water then gestured for him to get in. They did not join him, but instead shed their bloodied shirt, tossing it with Hiram's ruined clothes.

Hiram sank deep into the water, pleased by the scent it gave off; his nerves almost immediately felt less wound up.

Phaedrus sat beside the tub on the floor, resting one arm on the edge of the tub and their chin on that arm.

"You said you wanted to leave Pickering," Hiram said. "That it left a bad taste."

"Does that worry you?"

"Yes."

"Where you are, Hiram, that's where I'd like to stay."

"Oh."

"I would like to meet your family," they said, "if it isn't too much to ask."

Hiram sat up a little bit so that he could see the demon

more clearly.

"I didn't imagine you'd be embarrassed by me," they said, "At least not enough to keep me away."

"How could I be embarrassed?"

"By being as small-minded as most men," Phaedrus said simply.

Hiram smiled. "Will you always doubt me?"

"I haven't known you long, Hiram, perhaps a month? I can say with certainty that I love you, but the depths of your mind are as yet unknown to me. Give me a year or two, at least, before you scold me for having doubts."

Hiram slid back into the water, rested his head against the back of the tub, and said, his eyes on the creature, "I don't doubt you."

"You're very young, though, and perhaps a little stupid."

"Stupid enough to love you, I suppose."

Phaedrus chuckled. "I did that to myself, didn't I?" They leaned over and kissed him.

"What did you put in this bath?"

"Something to help you relax. Is it working?"

"It's making me drowsy."

The demon nodded. "Good. You should sleep. For a long time."

"How are we getting home?"

"Not on a coach!" the demon said. "Goodness, there has to be a way to get back without wanting to rip my hair out."

Hiram yawned. He fixed his eyes on Phaedrus' chest, looking at the small, crooked star that hung around their neck, resting against the green of their skin. "Would it be very bad to have a little longer than one lifetime together?" he asked.

Phaedrus gave a small smile and confessed, "I was a little bit more worried about how I would have to spend my lifetimes without you."

"Maybe it will be a good thing," Hiram said, not feeling sure but a little hopeful.

"We'll have to wait and see," the creature said with

sadness in their voice. "If it needs to be fixed, I will find a way to fix it for you."

He yawned again.

"Come along," Phaedrus said, taking him by the arm and helping him out of the tub.

Hiram felt small and young again as the demon toweled him off then lifted him up and carried him over to the bed. Phaedrus tucked him in under the covers and Hiram grabbed their hand.

"What?" the demon asked.

"You're not going, are you?" he asked.

"I was going to take my shoes off. I hope that's acceptable."

Hiram released their hand and they went, returning just a moment later to slide into bed beside him. They put an arm around Hiram's waist, and Hiram turned to nestle against their chest. The sensation of skin against skin brought Hiram a feeling of safety and peace he hadn't known in years.

"Ellen will like you," he said. "She likes stories. She likes *new* stories."

Phaedrus may have said something to him, but Hiram fell asleep soon after that and woke in the morning feeling light and warm. He had the strange idea, for a just a moment, that while he slept someone had come and turned him into a doll, taking away all his sore muscles and aching bones and replacing them with stuffing.

The demon had an arm around him and their forehead pressed between his shoulder blades; he must have rolled over in the night.

The creature pressed their lips against the back of his neck. "Are you awake this time?"

"This time?"

"You move a lot." They sat up and began to pull their hair over their shoulder, undoing the braid.

Hiram stretched a little too hard; the scar on his chest began to ache, and he looked down to see that bruises had formed around the area as well. Not fully awake yet, it took him a moment to remember what had happened.

Before he could dwell on it too long, Phaedrus leaned over and kissed him, moving their body on top of his after a moment. "Are you feeling well, Hiram?"

With blood thrumming through him and his heart pounding hard, he answered, "Wonderful."

"Good."

"Why?"

"I did say I had things I wanted to do with you once you were well," the creature said, "if you recall."

"What if I wanted to do something?" he asked, not with anything in mind but feeling he should add to the conversation.

Phaedrus laughed and kissed him. "Then we'll have to take turns." The creature pressed their mouth to the hollow of his throat. "Let me know if I should stop."

Hiram nodded.

After a few minutes of kisses, they turned aside the blankets and touched their mouth to his belly and then to his thighs. The demon took him into their mouth, and Hiram sighed, melting into the bed. He had thought about this often since the time they had been interrupted, and he had wondered what exactly he would do with his mouth when it was his turn to act in kind. It was advice that he couldn't have asked for, certainly not from Susan or Cassie; perhaps June, if he had been inclined, could have advised him in such things.

He forgot to worry about anything, though, for much of the time that Phaedrus moved their mouth along him, finding a harmony between the motion of their lips and tongue. Hiram finished, gracelessly, with a gasp and an odd, half-choked grunt. Though the demon still had their head bent over him, Hiram heard them chuckle and felt his cheeks flush.

Phaedrus sat back and covered their mouth with one hand, still smiling and said, "I'm sorry. It was a funny sound, though." They leaned forward and kissed his cheek. They wrapped their arms around him and held him close for a minute.

Hiram leaned into their embrace, his cheek against their chest.

"You almost made me choke," Phaedrus admonished. "It is polite to warn one's lover."

Hiram laughed, at first just a little, but then he couldn't stop. He pressed his head against the demon's chest, shaking with laughter. Phaedrus held him close until he calmed, and once he had, the creature kissed his temple.

It felt right to exist like this, as nothing but giggles and skin against skin.

Out of nowhere, after a few quiet moments had passed, Phaedrus said, "I should check on Mrs. Blackwell, though. In case her location had been revealed."

A little disappointed, Hiram asked, "Is that what you were thinking about?"

"Don't look so glum. I've spent plenty of time thinking about your mouth between my thighs," the creature said. They put a hand under his chin and tipped his face up, kissing him.

Hiram had imagined things like this. They had always felt like foolish daydreams. It had been a silly wish, to be held tenderly, to be cradled in the arms of another. "Would you like me to?" he asked.

"No, I'm content as we are," the demon said.

His eyebrows knitting together, Hiram asked, "Are you sure?"

"I will let you know, Hiram, if I want something, and I will tell you how I would like you to please me, but at the moment, I want this. I want to hold you."

"Oh."

"It's been a long time since I've had someone to hold," they confessed. "And...well, perhaps I'm a little nervous if you really want to get into it."

"Do you want to talk about it?"

"No."

Hiram nodded.

"It isn't something you should take personally."

"No, of course," Hiram agreed.

Someone knocked.

Phaedrus reached over and pulled up the covers, wrapping the two of them up like a cocoon. "Come in," they called.

Payton entered and said, "Not that I'm in any hurry to have you out of my home, but have you two thought of how you'll be going about your return trip?"

"A little, but we haven't come to any conclusions," Hiram said.

"Lovely. I have a proposal for you. We can discuss it over breakfast," she said and left, closing the door behind her.

"I suppose we should go to breakfast, then," Phaedrus said.

AT BREAKFAST they were joined by a pair that Hiram had never seen before; both appeared to be a few years his senior, dark of skin and curly-haired. They kept their dark eyes cast downwards, but when he glanced at them from the corner of his eye, their expressions were not as meek. Their hands were balled tightly at their sides.

"Runaways," he said to Payton.

"Perhaps," said his cousin.

There was no doubt in his mind that they had escaped from the South.

"What's your plan?" he asked her.

She examined her nails for a moment. "Hermes seeks passage northward, to Canada. As does Mary. Hermes tells me he served as a carriage driver in his previous life."

"You're going somewhere with this," Phaedrus said.

"I was thinking you could take our carriage—the old one, of course, Ian and I have a lovely new one—for your return home. With Hermes to drive. I don't imagine either of you can."

"I could," Phaedrus said.

Hiram almost laughed at the idea.

"Either way, your passage north has been secured," Payton said. "Considerably more comfortable than your way down, I imagine."

Hiram looked at his two new companions. Full of mistrust, discomfort. To his cousin, he said, "I'd like a loan."

She laughed. "A loan? I thought you'd resigned yourself to a punishing life of poverty."

"There's a venture I've been considering," he said, "on behalf of my niece. Who is your relation as well."

Phaedrus gave him a curious look.

"No need for persuasion, Hiram, though I am interested."

"A school," he said. "For Ellen, for others like her."

"Ah," Payton said. "Very well, a loan. You should pack. Speed is of the essence here."

"Are we not allowed to eat breakfast first?" Phaedrus asked.

"I don't know why you aren't eating already," Payton said, gesturing to the spread of food before them.

Phaedrus rolled their eyes and began to eat. Breakfast passed quickly, without a word from Hermes or Mary.

In the late afternoon, once they had packed and said their farewells, they left New York City, two sets of strangers. Phaedrus and Hiram sat in the back of the carriage with Mary, none of them saying anything. In his suitcase, Hiram had a loan from Payton and forged papers for their traveling companions showing them to be free people in his employ.

He tried not to gawk at Mary but she endlessly fidgeted, tense and seeming on the verge of tears. She caught him glancing at her.

He felt the need to say, "I've done this before. You don't need to worry."

Phaedrus glanced at him.

Mary looked up toward his face but did not make eye contact. She opened her mouth but closed it a moment later.

"Have you come a very long way?" he asked.

She nodded.

"It isn't too much farther," he said.

She nodded again.

"Is he...Hermes, do you know him?"

"My cousin," she answered.

He left her alone after that, not sure if she was worried or irritated by his attention. He examined his nails and found that they looked considerably healthier than they normally did; with one hand missing, he had not been able to pick at them.

That morning he had sent a letter along to Ellen, letting her know that he would be coming to retrieve them soon. With the immediate need to find Blackwell and the books gone, he realized he had missed the girl during his trip.

"What's this about a school, Hiram?" Phaedrus asked, pulling him out of his thoughts. "I didn't want to seem doubtful in front of your family, but I am curious."

"There are many freed people in our town. I can't be the only one who wants the best life for their child," he said. "And I'm sure there are many adults who'd like to learn what had been denied to them."

Phaedrus nodded. After a long silence, they said, "This carriage is a much smoother ride."

Hiram hummed his agreement and continued to look out the window. Though his task had been accomplished, something still weighed heavily on him.

They traveled until darkness began to fall and took lodging at the first inn they found. After dinner, Hiram and Phaedrus split off from the other two.

Hiram sat on the bed and began to unbutton his shirt, but halfway through lost his momentum. His hand dropped to his lap.

Phaedrus glanced over. "Do you need help?"

Hiram shook his head.

The demon returned to changing into their nightshirt, but when they had finished, they looked over again. "Hiram."

"What?"

"You're just sitting there."

"I'm sorry."

"No need for that," the creature said. "But...aren't you going to get ready for bed?"

"I..." He managed to lift his hand halfway to his chest but gave up just as quickly.

They came to sit beside him, putting a hand on his leg. "Are you feeling unwell again?"

He nodded.

Phaedrus put a hand to his forehead.

"No. Not like that. It's just...I've got this feeling in my gut," he said. "I feel as though something's wrong..."

The creature put an arm around him, pulling him close, and said, "A lot has happened. You need rest and good food and your own bed. You need your family. Here, let's get you settled, though."

They reached over and undid Hiram's buttons for him. They spoke soothingly to him as they undressed him and tucked him into bed, but Hiram found that even this could not quell the unease within him.

Once Phaedrus had settled into bed beside him, Hiram wrapped his around them and pressed close, his face against their chest. His chest ached and not just from the scar.

Phaedrus rubbed his back and said, "Whatever you need, Hiram, I'm here for you."

He began to sniffle after that.

"You'll feel so much better once we're home, I promise," Phaedrus reassured him.

"I'm frightened," he said.

"Of what?"

"Of what will happen."

"I'm not sure I follow."

"Everything is different," he said. "With you, with my family. Ellen...she's so young, and now I'll live to see her die..."

"What's different with me?"

"What will we do? How will we live?"

"How would you like to live?" the demon asked.

"Together," Hiram admitted. He didn't know if it was too

soon to say such a thing, but after so many nights with Phaedrus at his side, he didn't know if he could stand to sleep alone again.

"And you think I don't want that?"

"I don't know if we even *can*," Hiram said.

Phaedrus said, "I'm sure you feel very alone, Hiram, but people like you and I have always existed, and we always will. The world has room for us, even if it doesn't seem that way."

"I don't know."

"But I do," Phaedrus said, tightening their arm around him. "There's nothing to worry about. You need to sleep."

Hiram did not think that the creature was lying to him, but he began to cry anyway.

Phaedrus held him until he stopped, then wiped his face and kissed his forehead. "We'll be okay, I really think we will," Phaedrus promised.

Hiram dropped off to sleep not too long after that. He woke in the morning with the same feeling in the pit of his stomach. He did not look at Hermes or Mary as he climbed into the carriage, but he heard Hermes ask, "He sick?"

"He's melancholy is all," Phaedrus answered.

The demon came to sit beside him, followed by Mary. She gave Phaedrus a hard look and must have thought they hadn't been paying attention. When they asked, "What?" she looked startled.

She shook her head.

"You weren't staring at me like that for nothing," they said.

"Your skin..."

"Is green."

"Sure, but..." She glanced at Hiram. "He's white."

Phaedrus shook their head. "I can't be white. I'm not even human."

She gave them another long look, then nodded and said nothing else.

The carriage began to move.

Hiram nearly fell out of his seat.

The demon put out an arm to catch him and said, "You didn't sleep well."

"No."

"Come here. I'll tell you a story." the demon said, pulling him close.

Hiram rested against them, and Phaedrus continued to tell of Scheherazade's many nights entertaining her husband. After a while, a thought occurred to him, and he asked, "Phaedrus?"

The demon paused their story. "What?"

"Is she you?"

"Pardon?"

"Scheherazade. Is she you?"

"No, dear, Scheherazade bore her king three sons," they said. "And regardless of what experimenting I did with my form, I've never carried children. I'm sure that if I could, I would have by now, so I don't think I can."

Hiram sat up a little straighter and frowned for a moment, thinking hard. Eventually, he said, "Oh. Right."

Phaedrus laughed. "Right. It does rather preclude the issue."

Hiram shrugged. "I don't know, it just...I forgot."

The demon pulled him back to their side and kissed his hair. "You are a sweet thing, Hiram, really. May I continue?"

Hiram nodded, settling against the creature, not caring that Mary had begun to openly watch them.

AS ABOUT a week had passed, Mary and Hermes relaxed somewhat. Hiram thought it had to do with the demon's storytelling because both had commented on it at least once. One afternoon, when they had stopped on the side of the road for lunch, Hermes looked at the demon for a moment and said, "Mary says you aren't human."

"Correct," they said.

"What are you, then?"

"I was an angel."

The man wrinkled his brow. "Angels are green?"

"Certainly not all of us," they said. "Believe me or don't, it makes no difference."

They all ate in silence for a few minutes until Hermes set down his food and said, "If you an angel, can you tell me why—"

"Don't," Mary warned, her face serious.

"Why nobody answers my prayers?" the man finished.

Mary gave him a cross look, her lips pressed together.

"I'm not an angel anymore," the creature said. "I don't know how they run things in Heaven now."

"Nobody answers your prayers because you don't have any

faith," Mary told her cousin.

Phaedrus glanced at Hiram and quietly confessed, "I hate when people ask me about things like this. I never had any answers, even when I was in Heaven."

Hiram didn't know what to say. He looked up at the sky and around at the grass where they sat. "It might rain," he said.

Phaedrus raised their head a little and took a breath. "No, I don't think so. At least, I hope not."

The wind picked up a little, and Hiram imagined that it was a threat.

Phaedrus wiped their hands and stood. "I'm going to stretch my legs before we head out."

They walked away.

Hiram stood, cleaned his hand on his trousers, and hurried to catch up.

The demon glanced back. "You could have stayed."

"Oh, uh...I just...did you want me to stay behind?" Hiram asked, suddenly feeling that the demon must have wanted time away from him.

"No," they said. "I'm just going to stretch my legs."

Hiram hesitated, wondering if he should go back to the others. As he thought, Phaedrus continued to walk, glancing back after they had gone about two yards.

"Are you coming or not?"

Hiram had no answer and found himself rooted to the ground. He had not imagined himself as an insecure partner, but as he debated whether the demon's comment could be taken as rejection, the realization dawned on him. He had fallen for someone and found himself incapable of being without them. Being by the creature's side had become the only place that felt safe.

The demon approached and touched his forehead with the back of their hand. They took him by the hand and said, "Come along."

Hiram gripped their hand tight but did not move; instead, he pulled the demon back to him and buried his face in against their shoulder.

Phaedrus rubbed his back. "Take your time, dear. A lot has happened."

Hiram sniffled.

"Just breathe," the demon advised. "Focus on that."

Hiram took a breath and let it out slowly. He took another after that, trying to think only of his lungs and not of how it felt as though the world could fall away at any minute.

"You're okay, I promise," they said after a few minutes had passed.

Hiram nodded.

"This will pass," they said. "All of this."

"I'm sorry."

"Don't be. This is normal. I'd be more concerned if what has happened left you untouched. Are you ready to walk?"

Hiram didn't think he was, but he knew he should at least try. He nodded.

Still holding his hand, Phaedrus began to walk and when Hiram found himself frozen, they said, "One step at a time. Think about moving one foot."

Hiram took a single step and then one more.

Phaedrus smiled at him.

Together they walked for maybe a hundred yards, then turned back toward Mary and Hermes. Hiram tried to think about the movement of his feet, the pressure of Phaedrus' hand on his and the sound of the grass in the wind. He knew if he started to think about Blackwell, about his time in that basement, he would be back where he'd started. If he recalled the gouts of blood that had come from his hand, that had poured down his chest, he would be lost.

"What about you?" Hiram asked.

"Hmm?"

"Why isn't this happening to you?"

With a small smile, they said, "I imagine it would if I didn't have you to worry about."

"That doesn't seem right."

"And eventually I'll write a book about it. Maybe you

should try that, having a journal. Writing things down is an excellent way to deal with trauma."

Hiram almost scoffed at the word trauma.

"Ready?" Phaedrus asked the other two, who had finished their meal.

Hermes nodded and Mary gathered up the blanket they had shared. They all returned to the carriage, though this time Mary elected to sit out front with her cousin, the blanket tucked over her lap.

"Will you ever tell me the name of your book?" Hiram asked once the carriage had begun to move.

"Oh, of course, I won't," Phaedrus said.

"Why not?"

"Because I don't want you to know," the demon said. "It's my last secret."

Hiram made a face of doubt. "I'm sure you have many more secrets."

They shook their head. "No. Any other question you have, I'll answer."

Hiram studied their face for a minute, trying to think of a question that would test them, one that would pry, but he realized he did not care to know the scandals of their past. "If we live together—"

"When. We discussed this."

"You didn't seem to like my home very much. Dreary, I think was the word."

Phaedrus confirmed, "It's horrible, that gray little building. There's certainly no more room for another body."

"So where will we live?"

"I have an idea," they said, "But I won't tell you anything until it's finalized."

"That's another secret."

Phaedrus smiled. "It's not a secret. It's a surprise."

"Would you mind if we took a longer way home?"

"Why?"

"I thought we could visit Susan."

"Who is Susan?"

"Um...she cared for me when I was a child. I haven't seen her in a while."

"Oh."

"I'd like you to meet her," Hiram said, feeling bashful. "And we could pick up Ellen and the others while we're there."

"What's a few more days?" the demon said.

The carriage stopped, and they glanced at each other. Mary came around and opened the door, saying, "It's the border."

Hiram nodded and reached for his suitcase. He had expected this would happen. "I'll be out in a moment."

Phaedrus reached over and undid the buckles on the suitcase and handed him the papers from the top. Every morning he had made sure he could access those papers with ease. He exited the carriage with papers in hand and tried not to look nervous.

Two bored-looking men in uniform waited for him, and he greeted them pleasantly.

"Is there anyone else in the carriage?" one asked.

Hiram nodded.

"Have them come out, too."

"I've got all our papers here, though," Hiram said.

"Would you like us to get them?"

"No, of course not, one moment," Hiram said and took a few steps back. He opened the carriage door and said, "Can you come out?"

Phaedrus nodded, tightened their jacket around themself and exited the carriage. By now Hiram knew that this event could bring a level of scrutiny that would be painful for them. The demon drew themself up to their full height, their face losing some of its softness. Their hands gripped their jacket without any of their usual delicateness. Hiram had not noticed this behavior the first time they'd crossed the border.

The two men looked Phaedrus up and down; finally, one said, "Papers."

Hiram handed them over.

The minutes seemed to stretch into eternity as they waited. One of the men read each paper, settled their eyes on the person it belonged to and asked a variety of confirmation questions. Hermes and Mary gave short answers, their eyes downcast and voices meek.

Hiram nearly forgot his own birthday when it was his turn and had to explain that the loss of his hand was recent, so it wouldn't be noted in any of his travel papers. Each of the men looked at his stump, and he pointed out the newness of the scars there. They conceded the point and returned Hiram's papers to him.

They called upon Phaedrus last.

"Name?" one asked.

"Phaedrus Queen," they said, their voice flatter and deeper than it was normally.

The difference struck Hiram so badly that he had to look their way.

The creature did not meet his eyes.

"Date of birth?"

"January first, eighteen aught nine," the demon answered.

"Why are you green?"

"Copper mines," they answered. "It leeches into the water."

"Place of birth?"

"Atacama. That's in South America."

The man turned his eyes back to the creature's papers. The two guards leaned their heads together, whispering furiously. Finally, they handed back the papers and said, "Move along."

Phaedrus turned on their heel and went back to the carriage; Hiram stayed a moment longer to thank the guards, then joined them. The creature sat stiffly, even once they had moved past the checkpoint. They had their papers clenched in their hand.

Hiram asked, "Do you want me to put those away?"

Without warning they threw their papers onto the floor, breathing hard through their nose.

Hiram picked the papers up and tucked them back into the suitcase. He then turned to face the demon and said, "We'll have to go to get your papers fixed."

The demon glanced his way.

"Since they say the wrong thing."

They said nothing.

"But we'll be home soon. We can get it taken care of."

Their face crumpled and they put their arms around Hiram, burying their face in his neck. "I hate this."

"I know you do," he said, rubbing their back.

"Tell me it's just nonsense, Hiram."

"Of course, it is, Phaedrus," he said. "It's absolute rubbish."

They tightened their arms around him. "I really hate it," they said, tears in their voice.

Hiram kissed the side of their head and said, "I love you. I don't know what else to tell you except that it's a stupid thing you have to put up with and that I love you very much."

The creature sniffled, and Hiram felt their tears soak into the collar of his shirt. Hiram had not fully understood the gravity of their situation until then; no one had even asked to know their gender, but the very act of pretending, of avoiding the question had been too much. He did not know what to do while they wept, so he hoped that holding them sufficed.

When they finally pulled away, their face was wet, and their eyes were red-rimmed. They wiped their face with their sleeve, and Hiram offered them a handkerchief.

"Thank you. You're a love," they said, taking it, and dabbing beneath their eyes. "I must look a mess."

"You always look beautiful," he said.

They laughed, though it was not particularly joyful. "Flatterer." They wiped their nose. "I can't wait to go home."

Hiram glanced down, then said, "When June would say things like that, he always meant he wanted to go back to Heaven."

"No, I'd have no place there now," Phaedrus said.

"What was it like?"

"It's...well, it's hard to say. It's...have you ever been to the beach?"

"Not really. I've been to ports."

"You spent time at sea, though, didn't you?"

He nodded.

"Heaven is like the sea. It is great and deep and there is nothing one body can do to disturb it. There is no time. Everything is all at once and never at all. But when it has its upheavals, they are...monstrously large."

Hiram nodded. "I'll never see it, though, will I?"

"No one really lives forever, Hiram. It will just be a very long time."

"I meant..."

"Oh, not the, uh, the thing about not liking women," Phaedrus said, waving a hand dismissively, "That's got nothing to do with going to Heaven."

Hiram recalled plenty of things that had told him otherwise, but he did not feel it was his place to argue with an angel, fallen or otherwise, on such matters.

"Never been to the beach," Phaedrus said, "We'll have to fix that. The next time it's warm."

"It's never warm here."

Phaedrus smiled. "And we can bring your niece, and everyone will gasp at what a strange family we are."

"A family?"

"Of course. I am allowed to be part of your family, aren't I?"

"I hope so. We'll have to see if Cassie likes you."

"That's your niece's grandmother, correct? Your brother's mother?"

"Yes."

"Do you think she won't like me?"

"I've known her for my entire life, and I can't tell you safely that she will. I'm not even sure if she likes me most of the time."

"Oh?"

"Sometimes I wonder if she's just...it sounds silly, but I

think she feels bad for me. I was a nervous child, and my father didn't appreciate that much." Hiram shrugged. "If Cassie cares for me, then her heart is larger than I can comprehend, which it very well might be. Regardless of her feelings for me, she is a good woman."

"I'll have to settle for hoping she doesn't disapprove."

Hiram leaned against them, wondering if it could be as easy as that to become a family. To have Cassie glance the creature over and judge them instantly; she wouldn't say anything, but she would turn to Hiram and pat his cheek or arm. At least, that would be the ideal scenario. She would never say anything openly disapproving, but he would know by the way she looked at the creature.

When they arrived on Susan's farm, the first thing Hiram heard was the voice of his niece calling for her mother and grandmother, insisting no one else would ever come here, that it had to be him.

As Hiram exited the carriage, Ellen bounded up to him, nearly flying off the porch as she ran, but stopped short about six inches away. She stared up at him then looked at her feet, a hesitant smile on her face. "Hello, Uncle."

"Hello, Ellie," he said. He could think of nothing else to say. He had not spent so much time away from her since they had come to live together and seeing her again made him realize how awfully he had missed her.

She glanced up at him again, her hands behind her back.

He knelt, opened his arms and she threw herself into his embrace, pressing her face against his chest and squeezing him tight. He held her close and asked, "How have you been?"

"Bored!" she cried. More softly, she confessed, "I missed you."

He heard Cassie scoff from where she stood just outside of the farmhouse. The house, painted a buttery yellow, had rockers on the porch and enough room for a large family within.

Ellen pulled back and asked, "Can we go home now? We can, can't we?"

"Yes, but—"

"But what?" she asked, her eyebrows knitting together and her small mouth twisting into a pout. The expression only lasted for a moment because when she noticed Phaedrus, her eyes went wide and her mouth hung open.

"Someone new will be coming to live with us," Hiram said. "With me, more specifically."

Ellen snapped her mouth shut and looked back to her uncle, but her eyes darted back to Phaedrus. "Who?" Her eyes again strayed to the creature.

"This is my very good friend. Their name is Phaedrus," Hiram said.

The demon gave a small wave then folded their arms back against their body, uncomfortable and trying to pass it off as arrogance.

Ellen fixed her eyes on their face. "You're going to live with us."

Phaedrus answered, "Yes."

"You're friends with my uncle?"

"Quite close," they said.

Hiram stood and put a hand on their arm, hoping to soothe some of the snippiness out of their tone.

"Are you a mage?" she asked.

"No."

"What are you?"

"A storyteller."

She raised her eyebrows. "Do you know a lot of stories?"

"Thousands."

She looked at her uncle and narrowed her eyes. "Very good friends?" she asked.

"Yes," Hiram said.

She nodded, grabbed him by the hand and pulled him towards the farmhouse. "Auntie said to bring you in."

Hiram followed along, glanced back and tugged on

Phaedrus' sleeve when he saw they hadn't started to move. The creature started to walk, still not looking pleased. As they walked inside together, Cassie's eyes passed over Phaedrus.

"Have a seat," Susan said, not looking up from the garment she sewed.

Hiram sat, and Phaedrus took a seat beside him, their limbs still held close to their body.

Cassie, as she walked past, gave Hiram a pat on the shoulder.

Hannah reached out a hand to Ellen, and the child went to sit on her lap, nestling against her mother. She whispered something into Hannah's ear, and Hiram could only imagine what she said.

"Where's Flora?" Hiram asked. He glanced around and failed to see the woman with whom Susan lived.

"Out cutting wood," Susan answered. "Someone's got to do it."

"I owe you—" he began.

"I don't need to be owed when my friends come to visit," Susan said. She finally looked up.

"It looks like you've been well. The house is lovely," he said.

"Never thought I'd own something," she said. "You ought to stay. Eat something. Spend the night before you head back to that city."

"I don't want to impose."

"She already started cooking," Cassie said, "Killed a chicken this morning."

Hiram couldn't help but smile.

"Didn't expect so many," Susan said, "What's the story with those other two?"

"I don't know their plans for the future," he confessed. "I believe them to be runaways."

She nodded, then looked to Ellen and said, "Go invite them in."

Ellen scurried off, and once she was gone, Susan asked, "Where is your hand?"

Hiram almost laughed; he had not thought to mention it. "I cut it off."

All the women raised their eyebrows.

"Out of necessity, of course," he clarified. "But the situation has been neutralized. Nothing to worry about."

"I hope so," Hannah said.

"I wouldn't be bringing you home if I didn't think it was safe."

She nodded. She glanced over toward Phaedrus, who had hardly moved the entire time. She spoke in a carefully neutral tone. "And your friend...? Ellie mentioned you were bringing someone home."

Hiram nodded. "If you find it objectionable, the two of us can find residence elsewhere. I have no wish to make you uncomfortable."

"It's just that having a stranger around might not be so good for Ellie."

"Hannah, I would never do anything to risk her safety. Phaedrus is someone whom I trust very much."

"No, not that...it's, well, you know how she gets so attached to people."

Hiram's brow knitted. He had never thought of his niece as someone who became affectionate easily. Perhaps he had mistaken guardedness for detachment.

"She was broken up being away from you for a few weeks. Waited for your letters like it was Christmas, and she was so careful when she wrote back. Wanted you to be proud of her printing. I wonder if..." Hannah looked at Phaedrus again and then back to Hiram. "Just something to think about. Bringing in someone new. Someone who might not stay."

Not wanting to speak for the creature, Hiram looked to Phaedrus, who sat up a little straighter and said, "I have intentions to stay for quite some time."

No one said anything else for a few moments, seconds that stretched awkwardly until Hiram cleared his throat and said, "I'm opening a school. For her. For Ellen."

"Hm?"

"And for other children like her. Children whose prospects might not be what they should be."

"Children like her aren't going to have anything to pay you with."

"I plan to offset the costs by teaching magic as well."

"Teaching magic?" Ellen asked from behind him. She had come in without him noticing with Hermes and Mary in her wake.

"Yes."

She looked at her mother, eyes wide. "Mama."

"We'll talk about it," Hannah said.

"Please, Mama," she said.

"You gotta do your regular schooling first," Cassie said.

Ellen turned her gaze to her uncle. She said nothing, but he recognized the silent plea.

"You'll have to show me everything you've learned when we get home," he said. "I hope you've been practicing."

She nodded. "I read every day."

"And your sums."

"I practiced those," she answered with her eyes anywhere but Hiram's face.

"Every day?"

"Not *every* day."

"Hmm."

"I will, though," she promised.

"I hope so. You can't hope to be a mage without first being a well-rounded scholar," Hiram told her.

Flora returned inside after a while, bringing in an armful of wood. She gave Hiram a nod, which was the warmest greeting he'd ever gotten from her.

Over dinner, the mood around the table remained mildly uncomfortable. Phaedrus never relaxed. All Hiram could think was that they would have sore muscles if they remained so tense. After they'd eaten, Hiram couldn't stifle his yawns, and neither could Ellen.

"Head up to bed," Cassie said to the girl. "And you too," she told Hiram in exactly the same tone.

Ellen stood up and grabbed Hiram by the sleeve. "I'll show you," she said, "Nanny had me help her make the bed."

Hiram stood when she tugged on him. He looked to Phaedrus but found that Ellen had already grabbed them by the sleeve of their dress. The garment Phaedrus wore was not in any way modeled after current fashions, and the long, loose fit almost reminded him of a monk's habit, but the soft purple color, wide sash, and beaded trim transformed it into something more ladylike.

Phaedrus ogled the child for a moment, then stood and followed her.

As they walked up the stairs, Ellen and Phaedrus first, followed by Hiram, Ellen looked up at the demon and asked, "Do you think you'll live with us for a very long time?"

"I hope so."

"That's good. We don't have a lot of friends," she said.

"No?"

She shook her head. "No one who comes to visit ever wants to stay."

"I can't imagine why. You seem charming enough."

She looked up. "You said you know lots of stories."

Phaedrus nodded.

"Will you tell me one tonight?"

The demon hesitated. "I..."

"Please."

"I think a story would be just what we need," Hiram said.

"Do your stories have voices?" Ellen asked the creature.

"Pardon?" Phaedrus asked.

"Voices. Uncle always does voices."

"I can do voices," Phaedrus assured her. They glanced at Hiram.

Hiram smiled sheepishly. "It isn't right if you don't do the voices."

"Here I've been telling you stories with no voices. Shame on me," Phaedrus said. They touched Hiram's arm affectionately but drew back when they realized how keenly Ellen watched.

In Ellen's room, once the girl had burrowed under her covers, Phaedrus sat at the foot of her bed, and Hiram made himself comfortable sitting on one edge. The demon related a tale about a weaver girl and cowherd, and by the end, Ellen had nestled further into the bed and fallen asleep.

"She seems sweet," Phaedrus remarked as they made their way to the bedroom Ellen had pointed out earlier.

"She is."

"And bright. Doesn't miss anything."

"Apparently not."

They unwound their sash, then pulled off the dress to reveal thin silk underclothes. "You're staring," they reminded gently.

"Should I stop?" he asked, pulling his eyes away briefly so that he could shed his own clothing.

"I suppose it makes no difference."

"You're a wonder to me still, Phaedrus. I can't stop myself. Not until I know every freckle."

"Your family stared too, and I don't think it had to do with my freckles."

"Likely because they thought I would die alone," Hiram suggested. "They must be shocked."

At first, Phaedrus' face soured, but Hiram came over and took them by the hand, pulling them closer to the bed.

"But here I am, coming home with a lovely creature like you," he said. "They could never have expected this."

"I suppose not."

"Not to mention the hand."

"True."

"I'd also wager that they might have been staring at your jewelry," Hiram said, lacing his fingers through theirs and bringing their hand to his lips. "The last time they saw someone covered in diamonds and silk up close was before my mother died."

"I'm not covered in diamonds," they said, "The earrings are amethyst."

"Still. You are a fine, lovely thing, and we are...well, a

little shabby, these days."

"Perhaps they doubt my intentions with your virtue. It was intact when you left, after all," the creature suggested. "Perhaps they think I've bought your affections with coin and the promise of better lodging."

Hiram laughed.

Phaedrus slipped an arm around his waist and pulled him onto the bed. They tumbled Hiram onto the quilt and put one leg on either side of his hips. They leaned in to kiss him, and Hiram, struck by a thought, put up his hand to stop them.

"What do you mean better lodging?" he asked, trying not to be too distracted by the warmth of their skin beneath the silk undershirt.

"Hmm?"

"You said better lodging," Hiram said, "What do you mean?"

"Oh, that," they said and pressed their lips to his. "I've bought a house. Or, that is, I've arranged to buy a house. I imagine it might take some time for all the paperwork to be sorted. It was going to be a surprise."

"Phaedrus!"

"What?" the creature asked, their lips on his ear.

"You can't!"

"Why not? It's my money." They slid their hands up his arms and pinned him to the bed, firm but without any coercion. "If I want to buy us a house, I can."

"Yes, but..."

"But nothing, love," they said.

They kissed his throat, but when Hiram let out a sigh and arched himself to meet their body, they pulled back, moving off him to sit beside him.

"What?"

"I've thought better of it," they said. "We should discuss the house."

"Oh."

"It's a bad habit of mine," they admitted, "To use desire as a distraction."

Hiram pushed himself up and turned to face them. "I..."

"I won't make you come to live there, of course, and if you prefer that dismal shack of yours, I'll weather it, but it's a lovely house, Hiram. And I want to have lovely things with you," they said.

"I...it's only that I wasn't expecting it."

"That's why it would have been a surprise."

Hiram ran a hand through his hair.

"Besides, you can't expect anyone to send their child to learn magic from a mage who lives in a hovel," they pointed out.

"It's not a bad house!" he protested though he wasn't sure why. He had no fondness for the house.

"Ellen will love it," Phaedrus suggested, perhaps trying to sell the idea. "Her own room."

"No, of course, you're right about this."

"Have I upset you?"

He shook his head.

"Given you a terrible shock?"

"No."

"Do you feel faint?" they asked, a small smile playing on their lips.

Hiram could not help but smile. "No."

They reached out to smooth his hair from his face. "I love you, darling."

"I don't have the words," Hiram began.

"None of that drama or poetry," the creature chided. "There are three perfectly good words that have sufficed for every other pair of lovers. It is the way all my favorite stories end. I think we've earned that."

Hiram yawned. He couldn't help it. He shooed them off the bed and turned back the covers. He climbed in, and Phaedrus snuggled in beside him. Their fingers brushed across the scar on his chest, and then they pulled the covers up, making a small, safe world for the two of them to share until morning.

From the darkness, after Hiram had started to drift off,

the creature said, "I was expecting you to say, 'I love you' but don't feel obligated."

"Love you," Hiram said, most of his words lost in another yawn.

About the Author

Dan is an author and educator who has lived in Connecticut for their entire life. They received a degree in education and later wrote their Master's thesis on representation of women in same-sex relationships in contemporary Spanish literature and cinema.

What Everyone Deserves
2017 Rainbow Awards **Honorable Mention**
"Although the story deal with some real 1950's issues – discrimination, homophobia, interracial couples and hate crimes – it did it in a way that perfectly suited the characters and the story."
- Divine Magazine
In this 1950s period drama, Junius is a New York City fertility demon with a crush. Ever since falling from heaven he's been alone. Except for the mothers and children he watches over.

James Kelly Rosenburg, a black soldier with snowflakes in his hair, walks right into his life with a big problem. James Kelly, turned vampire during the war, is new to New York and its prohibition against vampire killing in city limits.

Junius offers to teach him to overcome his bloodthirsty instincts and live a proper Manhattan life. Their growing friendship leaves them both conflicted as they explore a city both welcoming and alienated by their kind.

That Doesn't Belong Here
"I liked the ... atmosphere that he created, alongside the paranormal creatures that roam the street. I liked that he wrote characters I could emotionally care for. If Ackerman writes another LGBT fiction, I will give it a try for sure."
*- Ami, **The Blogger Girls***
That Doesn't Belong Here begins when Levi and his friend Emily discover an impossible creature in an abandoned pick up. The thing is wounded, frightened and the two friends cannot leave him to the mercy of rubberneckers and tourists. This novel explores what it means to be a person, as the creature, Kato, begins to display not mere intelligence or friendliness but what can only be explained as humanity. The question of who we are allowed to love arises for Levi and Kato, as they are not just crossing the boundaries of gender or sexuality, but of species.